Cursed By Our Blood

Runway

To Anthony, Megan, & Marc-Anthony, I thank you for just being you. To my family and readers, I thank you for everything.

Introduction

Chapter 1

Everybody in Deer Island tried to keep up with the Joneses, ever did, always will. People in this small city were very familiar with what went on in others lives. They wanted to know what you had, what you wanted, and where you got it from.

Deer Island was a small city in the rural heart of South Carolina. Most out-of-staters had never heard of it. They didn't put it on the map until they found the biggest marijuana field ever growing alongside the bank of a river up there off of Hwy 69. Some said that it could not have been possible for old Mr. Tyson to grow all of that weed by himself. When they first found it, they discovered twenty-seven acres of beautiful tall plants. When they questioned him and asked him how he did it, Mr. Tyson said, "You know how we folks get greedy. First it was ten plants just to satisfy my needs, then ten became twenty-five, and twenty-five plants became an acre. When nobody saw the acre, an acre became ten acres and ten acres became all twenty-seven acres."

"People use to ask me all the time how I got all these fine things here that I have. I would tell them, I got my mind on my money

1

and my money on my mind. I meant that too, cause with this good pure stuff that I was growing here, my mind was always light and the profits that I got from "the goods" kept my money right!" They arrested Mr. Tyson that day, and to this very day he'll tell ya that he was the first and only true "King Pin" in the state of South Carolina. He would also make sure that you knew he was the one responsible for those people finally putting Deer Island on the state map.

Sylvia and John were both born in Deer Island. Neither of them had ever left the city as kids. In 1969, after Sylvia gave birth to Peter, whom everyone called Pete at the age of twelve, the old man, Mr. Kiser would not let her return back to school. Mr. Kiser told her that once you lie down and make a baby, you were no longer a child. You are now a woman. Women don't go to school my dear, a woman has to work! He made sure that Sylvia worked, too. Sylvia worked so much for Mr. Kiser that she hardly knew who was caring for her baby. She was like a mother lion in a pride. While she was out on the hunt, someone was caring for Pete's needs. Sylvia's childhood was swept from under her like a two dollar rug. All she was to Pete was a nipple to his mouth.

Sylvia knew that Pete longed for so much more. So, when Pete turned one year old and was weaned from the breast she allowed a couple a few blocks away to raise Pete as theirs. It pained her to do this, but at thirteen, what more could she give him when Mr. Kiser made sure of it that she didn't even have time to give her baby a mother's love. Sylvia heard through the grape vine that the couple she gave Pete to was unable to bear any kids of their own. The woman tried for several years, and to her accomplishment she had only managed to abort seven of the embryos that were successfully implanted into her uterus. Sylvia knew it the moment she

2

saw Mr. Kiser talking with Melvin and Patricia Riley, that this was the purpose for their visit, to see about her beautiful healthy baby boy. Everyone in Deer Island knew of Sylvia's condition, that she spent many hours in Mr. Kiser's fields, and was the queen of his still. Yes, before the age of ten, Sylvia was the best brew master to ever walk the Low-Country of the south. People came from far and near to get a taste of that spiritual grace. John would always say to her, "One day, you are going to be a well-known chemist," he was the only one that knew how smart Sylvia really was. Not even Mr. Kiser knew what the main ingredient in his moonshine was. People would ask and he would always tell them, "That will be one of my secrets that I take to the grave."

John hated the fact that he had ruined all of Sylvia's dreams. They were too young to be lovers. They were only playmates at the time. What they took as fun play turned into an addition that would forever change their lives. Luckily for the two of them, Melvin and Patricia allowed them to visit Pete. They said from the start that they had only wanted to do what they were told by God. Patricia told them of the dream that she had. God told her to take this baby, and show him the way to the pathway of heaven. This child was supposed to know of their natural parents as Jesus knew of Mary and Joseph. So with this known, the Riley's household was always an open door to Sylvia and John. John and Sylvia would meet there after John returned from school. They would play with Pete for a while and the rest of their visit was spent surrounded at the Riley's kitchen table. John would complete his homework while teaching Sylvia what he learned that week at school. He knew how smart Sylvia really was and did not want any wrong doings on his part to be the reason Sylvia didn't have the opportunity to learn as the others who were able to go to school. Even though slavery had ended, a man held a young girl captive in a time when many folks were celebrating and proud of their freedom.

The land on which Sylvia lived was very flat terrestrial. The dirt was black and the grass was green. As she stood in the middle of the woods blocked on all sides by pine trees and shrubbery watching the old rusty still steaming away, her mind wandered off from time to time. She couldn't understand why she didn't feel the same as things actually looked around her. On the outside she looked compassionate and strong, but on the inside she felt numb and weak. She saw the leveled ground, but she was overwhelmed by the deepness of the valley. Sylvia felt that low at this very hour of the day. She felt like the hills which she saw that could take her higher and away from this bitter world, were getting too hard to climb. All it took was the sound of a leaf passing by to snap her back into reality. Sylvia knew that no matter how low she was, no matter how hard the hills were to climb, she had to run. If she didn't make it out of this entrapment for her, then she knew that it would have to be for Peter. She wasn't there as a mother to Peter, but that did not stop her from loving her son. She longed to hold him from day to day, missing the feelings of his body when it use to move inside her. Just to imagine his milk breath blowing against the smooth of her neck was bitter-sweet. She hungered for her child, and when she couldn't soothe that hunger, Sylvia knew that she had only one option and that was to go before the throne of grace. Sylvia prayed for the Holy Ghost to comfort her and thanked God for his divine spirit.

Chapter 2

1940's
(Years Earlier)

Mary Dunlap was born a poor, unwanted child. The best thing that ever happened to her was when she met George Kiser. She remembers the day when George stopped and allowed her to shine his shoes. When he left, he gave her a tip and no one had ever done that. Mary was born out-of-wedlock to a mother of fourteen children. Mary was the last, and her mother thought that having babies was a thing of her past. Mary had never felt appreciated before, so when George gave her that extra nickel that day, she knew she had to have some more. Her heart was on fire. She'd never felt such emotions like this. Some would have told her that it was heart burn she felt, but she would have begged to differ cause she couldn't remember the last meal she had.

For weeks, George Kiser kept coming for a shoe shine. One day he asked her, "Do you want to go home with me?"

"Home with you for what?"

"Why don't you come home with me for a quick supper."

"Okay, I'll do that, but supper and that's that!"

Mary followed Mr. Kiser home that evening. He talked to her while he prepared a wonderful supper. They feasted on roast hen and sipped on wine. Mary wasn't use to this type of fine dining. When it was time for her departure, George asked just for a little kiss. He touched her on her neck and gave her a peck. George pinched her on her left nipple and whispered, "You are so ripe, can I have just a little bite?"

"No, Mr. Kiser. You invited me over just for supper, do you remember? I can't do this, I'm only sixteen. I can't be your lover. You are a man aren't you?"

"Yes indeed I am a man, twenty-six to be exact, but at sixteen you are a lady, matter of fact."

Mary trembling, "I can't do this. I'm not ready. I'm a Christian. I have to wait!"

Mr. Kiser being very convincing, "I want you to wait, but just for tonight can I just see what I've been missing? I won't enter you. I promise my dear, and I'll just make you feel real good. All I'm going to do is put it there, okay?"

Mary sounding not too sure, "I'm a virgin, never been touch. I don't think this is right. But if you promise to only do as you say then I guess it's alright. You have to hurry, cause I got to get home. Please don't trick me. If I let you touch me can I come back again for more supper? I think that I really like you, George."

Mr. Kiser said while lying Mary down, "If you let me Mary, you can come back for more than some supper, cause I think that I like you too." Once Mary had spread her wings like an eagle, George Kiser went all the way in. He didn't care that this poor girl never had anything stuck up her vagina. He went in and out like an amateur trying to plunge a stuffed up toilet. Not even the blood that he saw running down his shaft stopped him. To George, it felt so good, and he was going to enjoy it to the last drop, and he did.

Mary had never felt love like this. Mary had never felt anything besides hate before she met George Kiser. She felt like a queen, like someone sat her upon a pedestal. When George Kiser asked Mary to marry him, she said "Yes" before he could finish asking. Marrying George Kiser made her a happy woman. Her family that hated her before, all worshiped the ground that she walked on after she became Mrs. Mary Kiser.

Mrs. Kiser was impregnated instantly, because within nine months of her first sexual experience she gave birth to a healthy baby boy. They named him Paul. Paul was as gentle as a teddy bear. He never made much of a fuss. He was one of those babies that only cried when he was hungry and wet. To the Kisers, he was the perfect boy. He was just what George needed around his farm, Mr. Kiser would soon have a helpmate.

Within the next two years, Mrs. Kiser gave birth to another boy. This baby boy was much different than the first. He cried just to cry. Mrs. Kiser would tell everyone that she came into contact with, "I just can't seem to satisfy him. He cries all day and night. I make sure that he is fed and dry, but neither seemed to make a difference to Joseph."

She would tell people this, hoping that someone had an answer that would take her troubles away. This boy was a trip, at least that's what Mary would find herself saying for most of the day. She didn't know what to do with him. That old 'gripe' water didn't work that one of those old ladies at church told her about. Sometimes Joseph would just look at his momma's breast when she offered it to him, and cry out. Mr. Kiser would most of the time leave the house or retreat downstairs when Mary couldn't suppress Joseph's cry. Joseph's cry would sometimes trigger Paul to begin crying, and Mrs. Kiser would do the best that she could to comfort both babies alone.

Mr. Kiser did not take a part in the rearing of his children. He was like a male lion and he couldn't wait for them to be old enough to go out and hunt for him, so that he could get fatter. He knew that it took time, but babies would become boys and boys would become men. The more help that he had of his own, the less hired help he needed to keep around. He wanted his boys to be fed on cornbread and collard greens at an early age. At the age of six months, Mr. Kiser walked into the house, slapped the breast out of Paul's mouth and told Mrs. Kiser, "I don't want to see that boy sucking on either one of your tits again. Put a spoon in his mouth so that he can be strong and massive. I have never seen a weak Kiser man." So by the age of six months, both of the Kiser boys were eating from the pot and growing like Mr. Tyson's weed.

When the boys were old enough to run out of the house and play, Mary Kiser found herself knocked-up again. This time she gave birth to a baby girl in which they named Sarah. Sarah was born with a head full of curly, black hair. She resembled a baby doll that Mary never had. She was a quiet baby, much quieter than Paul. Mrs. Kiser prayed throughout this entire pregnancy that this baby would be more like Paul. Joseph was more than she could handle. If she could push Joseph back up her vagina, she would push him back up there and tell it to keep the change. She couldn't understand why the Lord sent such a wretch like Joseph. She had even considered changing his name to something a little more equivalent like Luther, which was as close as she could get to Lucifer. She just didn't understand how or why a child would do the things that Joseph would do. Mrs. Kiser really knew that Joseph was crazy the first day that she heard him tell his daddy, "NO!" Mrs. Kiser couldn't believe her ears. Her three year old had done something that she'd never done, but yet he was still standing. For some reason, Mr. Kiser liked the hardness that Joseph possessed. I mean, Mr. Kiser would take his side in an instant when anyone accused Joseph of wrong doings. Mr. Kiser loved this child. His inner spirit resembled Joseph so much that Mr. Kiser had pretended that Joseph would be the next king of his castle, not Paul his first heir. He even mentioned this to the boys time and time again. He told them at an early age that age didn't mean anything. He expected the same out of all.

Five years had passed, and Mary Kiser's baby girl had never spoken a real word. Both of her boys were talking by the age of two. So she found it mighty strange that her girl hadn't spoken a word. There were a lot of other issues that she was realizing about Sarah. Sarah did not like loud noises and she couldn't understand why her daughter walked about flapping her arms and hands. Sarah was also a biter, a very aggressive child when she wanted to be. Sarah continued to grow like a weed, but she couldn't say a mumbling word. Everyone that was close to Mrs. Kiser from the church would notice some of Sarah's inappropriate behaviors and would immediately begin to pray for her. Sarah would throw things at the boys, and she would even throw her supper at the wall. She was just frustrated, and not even Mary, her mother knew what to do about it.

One chilly, cloudy evening before Christmas, Joseph was ready to turn in early that night. For some reason, Joseph must have gone to bed too soon for Sarah. Sarah went behind him pulled his covers off and made some distracting noises. Joseph jerked his covers back on, popping Sarah in the mouth accidently. After being hit in her face, Sarah jumped on Joseph with all her might, and began kicking, biting, and scratching him until Mr. Kiser pulled her off of him. This was the day that Mr. Kiser put her in the very back room and told everyone, "Nobody better open that door to that backroom unless I tell you to. There's only one way to stop that dog from sucking eggs, and that's to get rid of the dog." Mr. Kiser knew that he couldn't get rid of Sarah, so he did the next best thing and he penned that bitch up.

Chapter 3

Mr. Kiser would soon find out that his son Paul Kiser wasn't going to be much help around his place. Paul was more than gentle. He was what most people called boys back in those days. He was 'soft.' Paul was so soft, that whenever Joseph would push him while playing, Paul would bend all the way over, practically touching his toes. Paul would even bend over during a game of tag if someone tagged him. One of the kids tagged Paul one day and yelled, "Tag, you're it!" Paul caught himself when he responded back, "If I'm it, don't just tag me, come and get me!" The young male child asked, "What's wrong with you, man? Come and get you for what? I just said you're it, gosh!"

Paul said, "Oops," and took off running behind the other children not even thinking twice about what had just happened.

At the age of eleven, Paul didn't realize what was going on with him. No one had ever told him why his penis began to swell in his sleep at night and why his underwear was wet and gooey when he woke up the next morning. No one told him and he didn't dare ask. He was still puzzled as to why he had gotten hair down there.

Paul had heard two of the older church ladies talking about him one Sunday morning. He recognized the fact that they thought

11

that they were whispering. Due to their old age and bad hearing, their whispers were like roosters crowing in the night.

The older lady said to her friend, "You can't tell me that boy ain't sweet!"

The other lady replied, "Now you know what they say about that. That's just an evil spirit and what we all should do instead of talking about Kiser's boy, is we all should pray for him. Pray for his deliverance from such evil spirit. He's young and unwise. He doesn't know what's wrong with him. We'd better be quiet because you know that they said Mr. Kiser shipped his daughter off to some expensive all girl school, because they believed something was wrong with her too. If you ask Mrs. Kiser, she'll tell you that they sent her to this school because she was so smart and they felt like the school here wasn't good enough for her. I'd believe that if we saw the child sometimes. That girl hasn't been here for Christmas, Easter, or Thanksgiving. Some would think that the child is dead. You looking at me like you forgot the girl existed, so I'll just stop."

When Paul heard all of this, he was so confused. He didn't know until now that people saw him as being different from other children. What confused him even more was the fact that these ladies thought Sarah was away in an all girl school. Paul knew that Sarah was where she always was, in that small, dark room at the very end of the hall. Paul knew this because it was his job to empty her bucket of acidic urine and stink feces. It was also Paul's job to clean Sarah up when she decided not to sit on the bucket in her room and instead she would go on herself. Sarah was not allowed out of her room, not even to use the one bathroom that they all shared.

When Sarah was sick, a nurse was called in for her care. Paul would always ask his mother when they were going to let Sarah come out of the room. Mrs. Kiser's response was always the same, "She will have to stay in there until she grows out of it." Paul wanted to know what "it" was. He knew that his sister only made loud grunting noises, but when he looked at her when there was daylight, she had the smile of a queen when he tried to make her laugh. Sarah's body looked like any other girl's body Paul had seen. So what was wrong with Sarah and how long would it take her to grow out of it?

Paul didn't know what was worse, not being able to talk, or looking like you're dying while trying to get out what you're trying to say. He often felt sorry for Joseph. Everyone at church said that he "stammered pretty badly."

Paul figured out Joseph a long time ago. Paul noticed that Joseph would rather get in trouble and be punished than having to talk to people, especially when he wasn't ready or didn't want to. The other thing that Paul knew about Joseph was that the boy stammered, stuttered or whatever those church people wanted to call it, but the boy could sing. He could sing, but didn't want anybody to know that he could. Paul would always hear his brother singing when he was doing his chores around the farm, and sometimes he would sneak into Sarah's room and sing "This Little Light of Mine." For some reason, Joseph thought that this song made Sarah happy. He was just sorry that whenever he snuck in there before bed time to sing to her, he couldn't see his sister's smile. Mr. Kiser had taken the light bulb out of Sarah's room, because he felt like all dummies belonged in the dark. Mr. Kiser told everyone living in his house, "If I ever find out that anyone put a light in there, that person will also get locked up in the dark with her. Sarah better be glad for sunny days and the light that she catches through her window. It's bad enough that I have to feed her dumb tail and give her a room to sleep in. She's better off dead!"

All of Mr. Kiser's children had some kind of issue, but there were certain qualities in Joseph that made Mr. Kiser love him more than he liked the rest. Joseph didn't fear anything besides talking, especially to non-family members. At home he would talk all of the time. His stutter didn't matter much to him around his family. He got use to his father laughing at him when he struggled to get his words out, and sometimes did it purposely just to make his father laugh. No one really got to see a smile on Mr. Kiser's face, so Joseph thought that it was impressive that he could do something that could nearly tickle his father to death. Mr. Kiser was tickled by the way Joseph's neck would stretch and his eyes would widen and close as he tried to get his words out. He would say, "Come on rooster, crow got damn it!" Sometimes Joseph would crow just for the hell of it, "Cock-a-doodle-doo!" Joseph was indeed Mr. Kiser's favorite. It didn't matter to him that Joseph would do the very opposite of what he would tell him to do most of the time. Joseph worked hard around the farm and that alone made him a good boy.

"Damn those teachers," Mr. Kiser yelled! It was the same week. Just a different day, and Joseph was still getting in trouble at school. He'd gotten a whipping everyday from the teachers, but it hadn't done Joseph or the teachers any good. He was constantly throwing objects at the other students or the teachers. He hated school and if that teacher called on him again to read aloud, Joseph promised that he would stick her right in her mouth. Joseph yelled one day as he was leaving school, "I-I-I-I-I will t-t-t-t-each yyyyyy'all that it t-t-t-t-akes m-m-m-more than a v-v-v-v-village to r-r-r-r-raise a child!"

14

Joseph couldn't read like the other kids but he didn't want anybody to ever know this. He thought that it was bad enough that he could hardly talk, but to try and talk and you don't even know the words, Joseph would rather cuss. Cussing was something that he realized escaped his mouth quite easily. It didn't matter what word it was. If it was a cuss word, he didn't stutter. So quite naturally he cussed all of the time. Joseph cussed young people, old people, rich people, poor people he would even cuss his daddy. Joseph was trying to figure this thing out for himself. If he sang, he didn't stutter. If he cussed, he didn't stutter. When he did read little easy books aloud in the bathroom mirror, he didn't stutter. So why did God make him stutter when it mattered most, when he really had something that he wanted to say? He figured if God was going to treat him like that, he'd rather be on the devil's side. It seemed to him that he'd be better off being on the same side that his father was on.

One day Joseph tripped an old lady and took her money and her mint candy. The lady looked up at him and told him, "Boy, you are going to hell!" Joseph looked down at her and said, "I don't care, at least I'll still be able to be with my dad if I go to hell. Why go to heaven and still have to see all you whack people that I don't want to be around now right here on earth. A one way first class ticket to hell coming right up and I don't want to miss that ride for anything else in this world. I'd give everything that I have to live eternal life with my father. So where he goes, that's where I want to go also. And everybody knows that my dad, Mr. Kiser, who owns Kiser's Farm, is going straight to hell!" With that he winked at the old lady and ran off. He didn't care that this woman now knew who he was, because he just didn't give a damn. He knew if she sent trouble his way, his dad would take care of it. For now, Joseph was four dollars richer and his blood sugar was going up because he had eaten all of the mint candy that she had in a little wrinkled brown paper bag which was balled up in her purse. He did think to himself, "Poor old lady, I'm sorry. I didn't mean to do it, but I did. Lord please forgive me." Joseph didn't know why he treated people so badly, and then felt sorry later when he thought about how awful he felt when his dad treated people so cruel, especially his brother and sister. He had questioned God many times, "God, do you want me to grow up and be like my father? If not, why do you allow me to do the things that I do and say the things that I say?" God never answered Joseph. He just made sure that life was tougher for him, and because of this, Joseph accepted that the answer that God had provided him was, "Yes, you are to be hateful like your father. Do as he does and say as he says."

Chapter 4

Sylvia

In 1957, Mary's fourth child was born. It wasn't a secret to most. Sylvia wasn't Mr. Kiser's child. Mr. Kiser and his wife had four children, two boys and two girls. Mr. Kiser was a blue-purple, slim fellow and his wife was a small petite dark-skinned lady. Three of their children fell in between, and then there was Sylvia. Sylvia was pecan-brown and thick. The little boys called her a "rump roast." They would say, "How come you are the color of the pecan and everybody else in your house is the color of the shell?"

People all around Deer Island knew how much Pastor Baker enjoyed Sunday Dinner at the Kiser's house after church service on Sundays. He would get very excited right after prayer time, because he knew that supper was coming soon. Pastor Baker was a red man in his early fifties, and he loved proving to the ladies of the church that age had nothing to do with it. He would tell them, "If God is for us, then who can be against us." The sound of his voice would make church women melt into his arms.

Well it turned out that Pastor Baker was visiting Mrs. Kiser for lunch on a regular basis. He would tell people that questioned his visits, "It's all in the Lord's work. My members are my sheep, and all good shepherds must tend their sheep." Poor Mr. Kiser was all about his plantation and his productions, so he was hardly ever near the main house during the light of the day. He knew of the traffic in and out of his house, because this was the most effective way of distributing his shine. Men would come and go from sun up to the risen sun of the next day. Through all of the comings and goings, the Kisers never fell short. They had all that they needed and all that they wanted. That was true only for Mr. & Mrs. Kiser.

Mr. Kiser knew that he had a problem that he just couldn't get right. When he was in his twenties and thirties everything worked downstairs. Mr. Kiser remembered turning forty and things worked great until the very last drop, which occurred within five minutes of entering the elevator doors. By age forty-five, Mr. Kiser felt like all he did was jumped into the elevator, pushed a button, and for some reason, he was pushed right back out. He didn't know what was happening, but he knew that he had to keep it to himself, cause he had never heard of any other man being casted from the inner doors. He felt sorry for Mrs. Kiser, because he could feel the urge of her wanting her buttons pushed. Her inner walls were moist and wet, but because of his disservice, he could sense the mildew and other deterrents he was causing to start lurking around. So he left her alone to satisfy her quench, but it was killing him that the mere sight of him didn't cause her to thirst.

It was indeed Mrs. Kiser that taught Sylvia how to pray. From the time that Mrs. Kiser found out she was pregnant with her fourth child, she was just a praying. Mrs. Kiser added a whole nother meaning to 'pray without ceasing.' That lady was scared. When I say scared gal, she was just a shaking, legs just a knock'in. If anyone said 'Boo,' she would have peed on herself. How would she explain to the world that she was impregnated by another man, and that indeed that other man was none other than Pastor Baker?

After finding out about her pregnancy, she tried her best to seduce her husband every chance that she had. Mrs. Kiser and her mister weren't as sexually active as they were in the past years. Mr. Kiser's limpness was just too much for her to bear after all of these years of settling. He was no longer attractive to her after she had laid with Pastor Baker. Now just the smell of his live stock on his skin was a reason for Mrs. Kiser to vomit. She recall the first couple of times that she ran to the restroom feeling nauseated, she blamed it on Kiser's smell. She later discovered her missed periods and this confirmed what she was praying against. She knew that her husband was no fool, but she sure wasn't going to give up and die without trying to at least convince this man that this child she was carrying was his. It took a lot of coaxing to get anything started between their sheets. She'll always remember all those long hours she put in stroking him with her hands and then polishing him off with her teeth. She compared her experience to kneading the dough to make bread. Mrs. Kiser just didn't understand why her husband wasn't turned on by his wife anymore, when she had another man that she couldn't turn off. Mrs. Kiser did her thing with Mr. Kiser for two months before telling him of their blessing from God. She even explained to him that maybe this child was the best thing that could happen to them to help them recapture what they once had. Mr. Kiser never looked at his wife the entire time while she told him all of this, and what sickened him even more was the idea that she told him all of this while sitting on top of him. Instead of her sitting there with him inside her with her lips holding him tight, there she sat as if holding a hotdog, because his wiener was just like that, resting right outside between her buns and nothing definitely could occur like that.

So, Mrs. Kiser's prayers were answered and Mr. Kiser never spoke a word. The beating that people suspect would happen, never was heard. Deep down inside, Mrs. Kiser knew that her husband knew that this baby that she called his was nothing to him and she meant so much less than any of their others. Mrs. Kiser realized while Sylvia was only a hand baby, that she could display no love to this child in front of her husband. She felt like the love that he saw displayed to Sylvia, was the same love that she shared with her secret lover.

Seeing Sylvia was a daily reminder to Mr. Kiser that he was a failure of what a real man stood for. She was more beautiful than anything he had ever reproduced, and smarter than those non-bastards all put together. He would always say to himself when he'd ask the others to do anything, "If I put my three seeds inside of a sack with Sylvia, she would sure come out first." He knew that they were some no gooders, but for some reason he tried to beat all of the good out of Sylvia, the bastard seed.

One day when Mary Kiser knew Mr. Kiser wanted to slap her, he slapped her baby instead. The only thing that she could do was call on Jesus and thank Him because the two of them were not dead. She knew very well that what she had done was wrong. Mrs. Kiser called herself a child of God and she knew that he was forgiving of all sins, so she went to him for forgiveness. She knew that she had yielded to temptation, and would she be tempted again? Probably so, especially if that preaching, praying, singing, shouting, Pastor Baker had anything to do with it. So she loved on Sylvia every now and again when no one, I mean no one could see. She would say, "I can't let no one steal my joy, not even you baby girl."

Sylvia knew that Mr. Kiser hated her. She felt like the more she pleased him, the more that he would like her, and her goal was for one day he'd love her. When she ran that still, Sylvia worked until her best was better, and her better was the best! But for some reason, Mr. Kiser had a hard heart. He didn't show a lot of love to the other three children or Mrs. Kiser, but Sylvia still noticed that whatever he was feeling toward her was all he had left at the very pit of his stomach. He treated her like the matter that ran through both of a man's intestines. It didn't matter that she was the source of their comfortable living. In his heart, Sylvia was the only physical thing that he had lost control of from the very start. Mr. Kiser tossed and turned many nights, just thinking about another man stirring around in his hot porridge. He knew that he went out to take a walk in the forest, thinking that it was safe to leave his porridge cooling on the table. But to his rude awakening, when he got back the porridge was just right, but someone had already eaten most of it. It hardened his heart to the world.

Sylvia continued to do right by Mr. Kiser. She herself called him Mr. Kiser, because he had never treated her liked a dad. She knew that Mrs. Kiser was her momma, but no one had ever told her that Mr. Kiser was her dad. She sensed this as a baby in her cradle that someone had gotten this thing wrong, but all she could do was listen to her mother's song. Her mother would always sing to her: "Hush little baby don't say a word, momma's gonna buy you a mockingbird. If that mocking bird don't sing, momma's gonna buy you a phone that rings." Sylvia was smart enough to know that momma's word for her was not the same words that she sang to the others. So, Sylvia knew from the cradle that the man that the others called daddy was not her Pappy. She just called him Mr. Kiser, because if she called him Daddy and he said, "I ain't ya Pappy!" Sylvia would die.

Chapter 5

John

John left two days ago and Sylvia's eyes hadn't been dry since. She knew that this day was drawing near, but to see him leave felt like a tragedy within her soul. This was now the second person in her life that mattered most that she had to let go of. Sylvia believed in "Let Go and Let God," but God, when are you going to do something? She cried out, "Lord, do something for me, right now!"

It was 1971. John turned eighteen a few months ago. He had discussed this with Sylvia for years that leaving was the only hope that he saw for having any sort of future. So he had to join the Army. John knew since they were young, that this was when his and Sylvia's four year age difference was going to have an effect on their lives most. John was only sixteen when he fathered that child with Sylvia. Some people said he should have been sent away for bothering that little girl and getting her pregnant that way.

John had known everything about the birds and the bees ever since he could imagine. He watched his father and uncles bring women into their small two bedroom house night after night after night. They would fall wherever they may, and wherever they fell was where they would lay. John had seen the aggressive, impulsive act of sex too many times, that he now ignored the moans and groans of whoever laid beside him. John's father or uncles didn't care that he was only an innocent little boy who had lost his mother to domestic violence. They only cared about that squirrel between their legs that was trying to get a nut. Once they got that nut, they were concerned with rather they could get a few more nuts before the harvest ended. The men in his family were very reckless men when it came to women. They only wanted one thing from a woman and once that need was met, "good riddance." Just like the woman that John's father, Mr. Jones brought in his bed now. He brought John's mom there too a couple of years ago. Mr. Jones laid with her all night long, but before daylight could show its face, he dropped her off where they met the night before.

Mr. Jones was angry when Doris, John's mother showed up on his doorsteps and confessed to him that she was pregnant with his child. He told her that it couldn't be, he'd only known her for one night. She laughed right in his face, spitting and all, "That's right, one night, and that was one night too many." The horrible smell of alcohol confirmed that she was probably drunk. Mr. Jones couldn't understand how any baby could live through all of that! He said to himself, "It's gotta be a strong man, a Jones Man at that!"

Mr. Jones did right by Doris and married her 'shot gun' style on a cloudy Sunday evening just one week before John was born. Mr. Jones prayed about his current situation and decided that no matter what, he did not want any bastard kids. He had grown up with many kids who didn't know their fathers, and he felt like they were all missing a huge chunk of the pie. He knew that he was very far from being perfect. But his bastard friends, screws were so loose, that they couldn't hold on to nothing. He just felt like they had nothing to offer, no brain at all. Mr. Jones would always say in comparison to their brain, "Someone is home, they could have light, but no one paid the light bill." So due to this realization, he did not want a bastard child, not now, not ever, even if it meant being with Doris.

After John was born, Mr. Jones tried his best to be a good husband to his wife. To his surprise, Mr. Jones found out that Doris was nothing but a bastard herself. Doris didn't know anything about anything. She had earned her way through life's toils and snares by opening her thighs and flooding her gates. Most men that she'd been with hunted her down, because they said when those gates opened, she would rain down on them. One man said, "The damn levees broke. Save me! I believe I went in and now I can't get out!" She was a 'Dime.'

Married life was becoming exciting for Mr. Jones. He was starting to believe that all things did happen for a reason, and this reason was starting to feel good. He loved coming home from work to see his baby boy and mommy resting peacefully in his castle. He didn't know that this feeling was possible for a black man living in a small city like Deer Island.

What Mr. Jones would soon find out was that Doris was not a full closed purchase. She was only a lease with an option to buy. That's right, Doris was a dirty filthy bastard. No one loved her, so she had grown accustomed to only loving herself. One night after putting it on Mr. Jones real, real good, this heifer got up and said, "I'm sorry Baby, but I'm not cut out to be nobody's wife. I tried to make this work, but being a mommy and being a wife is just not cut out for me! I'm just so glad that I don't have to leave you all here alone. You can have my sweet little boy Johnny, cause he is all yours now. I'm sorry, but what else do you want a girl to do. I have to go and be about my brother's business, because he is my pimp you know, and I am definitely my brother's keeper. So long now Baby. You know where to find me when you want to take this thing for a ride."

Big Johnny, as Doris would call him, had never felt so hurt and betrayed. He vowed that another woman would never come close to his heart. What was he going to do with a baby? John was now four and knew his parents' comings and their goings. But this absence of his mother was one that he couldn't understand and his daddy didn't know how to explain it, cause he was lost his damn self. He went day in and day out trying to convince himself that he had done nothing wrong. What it is was what it is, and there was nothing that he could do about it. There was one thing about a Jones man. They'd bounced back from time to time, but they sure as hell knew how to bounce forward. They prepared themselves, because they knew that the storm was just passing over.

Mr. Jones was glad he had prepared himself, because it wasn't one month since Doris left him when he got the news. The officers pounded his door down one night and shined flashlights through his window. His first act was to protect his son. So, he covered his sleeping child in a blanket and tossed him to the floor. When he opened the door, they handed him what looked like a women's purse. The words that he heard next would rest with him for the rest of his life, "Sir, your wife is dead!" With those words said, Mr. Jones heard his only child scream from the top of his tiny lungs, "NO, I want my momma!"

They later found out that Doris was shot in the head by a former lover. Her good loving ended up being the poison that drew her in. She closed her eyes and slipped out of life's backdoor, leaving behind a husband and a small child. Doris came into this world and left this world never knowing who her father was. Some said that this was the void she could never fill. Doris had never turned down an opportunity to jump on a man, wrap her legs around them tight and tell them to giddy up, but before she got up off of them, she looked them deep in their eyes and asked, "Are you my Daddy?" Would she have still been alive if someone had just said, "Yes?"

Chapter 6

1973

It was the morning of Sylvia's sixteenth birthday. Since Sylvia had given Pete away to the Riley's, Mrs. Riley allowed Sylvia to spend the day of Sylvia's and Pete's birthday with her child. These were the only two days in the year when she would be left alone with her child for at least six hours. On these two days, Sylvia was always overflowed with joy. Pete would be turning four years old in a few months as well. No one could have given her a better present than this, not even John. John was away serving our country, but he hadn't forgotten Sylvia's birthday either. Sylvia's package was received two days ago. Along with her gift was a long letter from John encouraging Sylvia to stay strong. He would always tell her, "And this too shall pass." In a small box, lying beside the letter ticked an antique pocket watch. When Sylvia opened the beautiful watch, there it was written: "I'll love you until the end of time." She cried, closed her watch, placed it in her pocket, and went downstairs.

To Sylvia's surprise, she just knew that her mother would be waiting with her secret hug and tender kiss. Her mother was nowhere to be found downstairs. She had never left the house without at

29

least blowing Sylvia a kiss. This was the only moment of their day when they acted as mother and child. Mrs. Kiser purposely treated Sylvia like a step-child throughout the day and night, because she felt like that was the only reason why Mr. Kiser never made a fuss about her.

Outside, Sylvia continued to look for her mom, but her mom was nowhere to be found. She knew that she was wasting time that was supposed to be spent with Pete, but finding her mom was of great importance today. Mrs. Kiser had always told Sylvia that a little girl's sixteenth birthday was a special birthday indeed. So Sylvia waited for this day for a very long time, wondering what was going to happen, hoping that it would change her life forever.

After hearing noises at the barn, Sylvia ran over that way. Mr. Kiser called to her from a distance. "I'm going to need you to get to work young lady. I just got in a special order. I need three cases of shine ready before sundown."

"Not today, Mr. Kiser. Did you forget about my birthday?" Sylvia questioned.

"Your birthday, who cares about your birthday? The sperm that made you should have been spat out your mother's mouth or jerked off in a tub or something! Don't you ever remind me of your birthday or any other day. You just get your behind out there and make my shine! I don't want no weak shine either, you hear me! I want you to brew that juice that always makes them come back for more. So get going, you bastard," shouted Mr. Kiser!

Sylvia could hardly walk through the woods that morning. Her legs felt like it was going to give out on her. She felt beaten and torn. She saw the old copper still waiting ahead, but today for some reason, it looked different. It looked as if it had horns, eyes, and a tail. Sylvia had never outwardly questioned God, but today she screamed out, "Why me Lord?" After receiving no answer, Sylvia pulled out the corn meal, sugar, water, yeast, malt, and her secret ingredient. She cried realizing that she didn't even get to tell Mrs. Riley that Mr. Kiser needed her on today. She knew that Pete was anxious to see his momma. She knew that he knew she was his mother, even though he called Mrs. Riley momma. She assumed that it was something about a mother's smell that a baby never forgot. She could tell by the way her son held on to her. He held her like a permanent attachment. Her heart was heavy.

While tending the still and watching the steam carefully, Sylvia couldn't help but cry. She couldn't understand why Mr. Kiser would take something as precious as visiting with her child on her birthday from her. Her eyes were filled with tears and the air around her was filled with sobs. Sylvia was so overwhelmed that she didn't notice the slop leaking from the still. Another step forward and Sylvia would soon realize this while gasping in severe pain, because some slop had fallen on her right foot. Sylvia hollered in pain. Just like grits, the slop stuck to her skin. Sylvia wasn't wearing her rubber work boots as usual because on this day, she was supposed to spend it with Pete. "Help, help," Sylvia yelled. She was now on the ground trying to use some moss from a nearby tree to wipe the slop off. After seeing her own skin peeling, she almost fainted. Was this just too much to bear all alone? This time instead of calling out to God, she called out to John, "John, where are you when I need you most?"

Sylvia was frightened by steps approaching her because she knew that she was defenseless lying there on the ground. She didn't know if it was a man, bear, deer, or wild hog. She could tell by the steps that it was heavy. As the steps got closer, she could smell the scent of Mr. Kiser's pipe. At least he wasn't as bad as something she had imagined.

Mr. Kiser yelled, "Are you crazy, why are you making all of that noise? Do you want somebody to find you and my still back here and get us both locked up? Get up off of that ground slut. You are really working my nerves this morning. My birthday, my birthday! You know what, you know what, Mrs. Fast Behind? Do this for me since you thought that you were a woman long time ago. Mr. Kiser zipped down his zipper and pulled out his penis. Come here right now. Bring your behind here and blow out Big Daddy's chocolate coated candle, since it's your birthday. Did you hear me, Sylvia? Get over here!"

Sylvia couldn't move, she couldn't believe what was happening to her. First no visit with Pete, and then she burned her foot. Now Mr. Kiser wanted her to put his private parts in her mouth! What was she going to do? At that time, Mr. Kiser picked up a stick and threw it at her. She slowly crawled over to him, looking at something eye to eye that she had never seen before. Strangely enough, when she was with John she had never seen his. She had never seen it because she was afraid of it. John would always tell her to close her eyes, as he put it in. And now today when she had already confessed that she needed John most, it seemed like the hills were getting harder to climb and she just wanted to let go. She felt like it probably felt better falling way down than being up where she was doing what she was about to do. She looked Mr.

Kiser in his eyes and knew that if she didn't put him in her mouth, he was going to kill her. Mr. Kiser grabbed Sylvia by her hair and guided himself gently into her mouth. At first she just knelt there, after a minute had past, Mr. Kiser hit her side her head and told her, "Do it, you little bastard!" Shortly after being hit side the head by Mr. Kiser, Sylvia's mouth was filled with a white chalky paste. It smelled of bleach, but she knew that it couldn't be. As soon as she motioned to spit it out, Mr. Kiser grabbed her throat and said, "Swallow it, you little tramp!"

When Sylvia assumed the worst was over. Mr. Kiser pulled down his pants, he pushed her back and told her that he was going to make her beg for more. He said, "I've been watching you. Your behind and breast have been getting bigger, your thighs look like creamy caramel, and I'm sure that you're as good as your shine. I know that you like this Sylvia. You've proven that much, bringing some baby in this world before you knew how to pee straight. You wanted to know if I had forgotten your birthday. Don't worry, I didn't forget at all. I've been waiting on this day for a very long time. I know by now you've heard that I may not be your father. Well the only reason that I didn't put you and your momma out of my house was because she made me a proposition that I couldn't refuse. She told me that when you turn sixteen that I could make you mine, all mine. I could have you any way that I liked. She told me that she could be my milk and that you could be my honey. Looking at you every day was hard for me. I've wanted to get between these plump thighs of yours since Peter was a baby. The way that Peter would pull on your breast would make me wet in my pants. You are so succulent and sweet. Lay back my child, and let your daddy finally get to hold his baby. And don't worry; daddy is going to take care of his new baby girl."

As Sylvia lay there with her eyes closed, she couldn't feel a thing. Her body had gone numb. She could no longer feel the burn on her foot, only her heart beat. She was paralyzed by the thought that what she had waited on all these years and had hoped to change her life, something her mother told her was going to make her feel special, was right there on top of her, her worst nightmare. This time Sylvia had fallen and couldn't get up. She had longed for this man to show ownership of her and know she was his little girl. Sylvia cried and cried, but to her satisfaction, Mr. Kiser wasn't on top of her long. If she had counted, one Mississippi, two Mississippi, three Mississippi, four, he would have been done.

Chapter 7

It was one of the coldest Christmas Eves ever on Deer Island. The snow storm surprised everyone this winter. They hadn't seen snow in over ten years and even then, it was only a sprinkle. The snow covered the grass. Everything outside had turned white. It was such a lovely sight. The children couldn't wait until the storm cleared so that they could build their first snowman. Paul stood Sarah to the window, making sure that she got to witness what he and Joseph thought was the best Christmas Eve ever. Sarah too was very excited by the snow. The boys didn't know if she knew what was happening, but they knew that the sounds that were coming out of her mouth was quite different from the usual grunts and screams. She seemed more at peace as she watched the flakes fall through the window. The boys so wished that there was a way to sneak Sarah outside, so that she could experience this first moment with them. They knew that Mr. Kiser was nearby tending to his livestock. The animals were very noisy this particular evening, probably due to uncertainty of what was going on out there.

Right before they could leave Sarah's room, they heard the back door slammed. "Paul, Paul, come on out here. I need your help," yelled Mr. Kiser. "Why y'all shut up in that room with that thing. Get out here. I told y'all that what she has may be catchy. If

35

that curse jumps on y'all, I swear that I'm not keeping you around here. One of them is too much."

"We're coming dad, just let us put on more clothing," said Paul.

As the boys followed their dad outside toward the barns, they could hear the pigs squealing. They heard squealing before, but as they got closer these squeals were frightening. "I wonder what's going on. It sure doesn't sound good," said Joseph.

"Get over here, Paul," yelled Mr. Kiser!

When Paul got closer he saw where the loud squeals were coming from. There was a huge hog lying on its side. It was kicking and frothing at the mouth. Paul had never seen a hog like this. All of the pigs that he'd seen lying down looked so peaceful. This hog looked like it was fighting for its life, but Paul couldn't see what it was fighting against. It was angry, completely deranged. He hadn't realized until now how many teeth hogs had. Joseph looked like he was trying to get closer to the beast. Paul was backing further away. Paul now knew why he'd rather stay in the house and take care of Sarah, than being outdoors taking care of his dad's animals. This was just too much.

"Paul, get your ass down here behind this sow! She's going to die if we don't get these pigs out of her. Why you still standing there, fool? Take that big coat off and kneel down here. You might as well get that look off of your face because you about to look into something that looks just like your mouth in a minute. My hands are too big so I'm going to need you to slowly put your hands up her and pull them damn pigs out. Something has gone wrong and she can't bring them on her own." Mr. Kiser was furious.

Paul couldn't move. He couldn't believe what his dad had just said. Did he just say that I had to put my hand into that sow? Oh no, I'll die first. "I can't, I can't do it. There's no way. That thing will bite me. She's bleeding, look at the blood. Oh my God, please save me!"

My Kiser got up and pushed Paul to the ground. In one snatch, he pulled off Paul's winter coat. Joseph was scared now because he knew that if Paul didn't do as his dad said; Paul was going to regret it. Joseph knew that this was something his brother couldn't do. He had seen Paul soak his hands after emptying Sarah's bucket. So he knew Paul was going to throw up if he had to put his hands in that blood bath.

Paul could feel the heat from the pig as he stared at it. Mr. Kiser was now putting pressure on the sow ensuring that she didn't snap back and attack Paul. The pain of trying to deliver had her weak enough for Mr. Kiser to hold her down. There was froth and blood all around them. Mr. Kiser really didn't think the sow was going to make it, but if he could save her litter of piglets that would indeed still be a blessing. This old sow had delivered one too many times during her lifetime.

After a few minutes Mr. Kiser had really grown tired of his elder son. He took Paul's right hand and rammed it up the sow's vagina. "Pull those pigs out you faggot! I guess since Sarah can't be a daughter you have decided to take her place," yelled Mr. Kiser! Paul had nearly fainted at this moment. His hands were buried inside of a hog's vagina. He could feel the movement of her babies inside her and at that instant he did faint. Mr. Kiser looked at him and said, "Weak! Joseph, get your butt down here and pull these pigs out of this sow. Your hands are small enough. I just wanted to see if your brother could do it!"

Joseph helped Mr. Kiser move Paul out of the way and then he kneeled down behind the sow. There was even more blood on the ground than before. Even though it was cold outside, Joseph was sweating like a bull. The squealing of the pig and the anger of Mr. Kiser had his adrenaline pumping. Joseph got down where he could smell the sow. He rolled his sleeves up and stuck his hands deep inside. He didn't realize that in there was going to be so warm and moist. He actually liked what he felt as he moved his hand around trying to grasp the piglets so that he could pull them out one by one. Joseph couldn't believe it. Every time he pulled out a piglet, it seemed like another one surfaced. In all, Joseph pulled out eight live pigs and he fished around some more and pulled out three dead piglets. When it was all over, Joseph looked at his hands at the same time feeling the warm, wet feeling in his pants and said, "Wow!"

Mr. Kiser and Joseph cleaned up everything and placed the piglets close to their mom so that they could nurse from her, because it was going to be a long night. Mr. Kiser knew that if the sow didn't make it, he would have to feed them by bottle tomorrow. He sent Joseph into the house to wash up and told him not to come back out. He kicked Paul and called him every bad name in the book. Mr. Kiser expressed how regretful he was to have a sissy for a son. He said, "I knew that Joseph was man enough to help the sow deliver her piglets, but I wanted you to prove me wrong. You couldn't do that at least once. You walk around here switching your tail looking pretty. What's wrong with you boy? How did you turn out this way? I have never heard of a Kiser man being anything less than a man!

Do you know what men do to punks? Do you know what happens when you live in a city and people think that you're a faggot? You are a disgrace to our family. You have made me shame."

Paul sat with his face in his hands. He never wanted to hear his father say these words. He loved his father and did not know what people saw in him. He tried to be like most men he saw. He thought that he was finally doing a good job at it. His dad caught him completely off guard today. He had never imagined putting his hands anywhere close to there. If only he hadn't fainted, he could have done what his dad wanted him to do.

Mr. Kiser knocked Paul up against his head. He didn't know what became of him at the moment. He pushed his oldest son against the wall of the barn and yanked his pants to his ankle. He screamed into Paul's face, "If someone is going to do this to you, got damn it, I'm going to put it to you first!" Mr. Kiser pushed his son harder against the wall while pushing himself deep inside of him. Paul squealed liked the sow and his butt bled like the sow. Through all the pain he felt, he had never imagined being raped by his own dad. As he felt his face against the cold boards his insides died that day. As his insides died with every thrust from Mr. Kiser, Paul looked down at the old sow and saw the life in her slipping away as well. He realized then that they both had experienced similar acts on this Christmas Eve. He could only think that Joseph's hands moving in and out of the sow had to feel quite as painful as Mr. Kiser moving in and out of his first born son. Where was Jesus when you needed him most? Could it be that he was getting ready to celebrate the anniversary of His birth? What a white Christmas this was turning out to be!

Chapter 8

1974

It was Pete's fifth birthday. Sylvia was very excited about helping Mrs. Riley decorate for Pete's birthday party. This would be the first time that she got to spend the day with them since Mr. Kiser made her miss her visit on her sixteenth birthday. Her heart still yearned to be with her baby after all of these years. At this point in her life with John being gone, Pete felt like all she had. She dreamt of kidnapping her own child and running far, far, away. The only reason why she had not was because she knew that she wasn't living a fairy tale. Her life was pitiful and she often pretended that she was living a fairy tale. She couldn't keep Mr. Kiser off of her and she cried day and night knowing that her birth mother listened to her husband thrusting in and out of her and she never muttered a word. Many nights Mr. Kiser would call Sylvia into the bed with him and Mrs. Kiser and he would make her mother watch as he went inside of her. How awful, Sylvia thought. If the experience was that painful to Sylvia, she wanted to know deep down inside how her mother felt lying next to her. How can one man be so hateful? Why was God allowing good men to die in the war and allowing this creep to live like a king, so he thought. When Sylvia wasn't praying for Mr. Kiser to die, she was praying for John to live.

41

John had been fighting the Vietnam War for a time now and Sylvia worried about waking up one day to learn that the only man that ever loved her was dead. John had written her a few times and she had written him back. He was scared of dying at a time when he knew that he had to live. He had promised Sylvia that he was coming back. He had to come back. If John didn't come back alive, he knew that Sylvia would be miserable all the days of her life. He hated that Sylvia had hinted around of someone causing her pain and suffering when she wrote to him, but she wouldn't tell him anything in great details. He knew that her hurt wasn't just from missing Pete. He knew Sylvia too well. She wasn't going to tell him who hurt her so the best he could do is keep fighting making sure that he came back to Deer Island alive.

Sylvia knew that she couldn't tell anyone about her and Mr. Kiser. She was already hurt by it, if anyone found out she would also have to deal with the embarrassment. Living with a man that she hated was tough. Living with your mother, who set you up for all of what you were going through was horrendous. Sylvia sometimes felt like flying. She felt so empty that her body felt like it could just float away. The only thing that got her through was that she'd heard an old lady in the church say to a battered wife, "Just call on Jesus, He's the only one that can and will save you." So Sylvia did just that and she called him until she felt something taking over her, "Jesus, Jesus, Jesus, Jesus!"

Mrs. Riley had told Sylvia to come over to her house by nine o'clock. Sylvia was not going to be late. She'd said to herself the night before, "Lord, if Mr. Kiser does anything to try and prevent me from being with my child tomorrow, I'm going to have to kill him." She was so afraid all morning that he was going to attempt something. He was just that hateful. Sylvia ran out of the house before anyone could ask her to do anything. She was up since four o'clock doing every chore that she had ever been asked to do all the time making sure that no one could sabotage her day. When she saw the Riley's house close by, she could only give God the praise.

Peter looked like he had grown at least five inches taller since she saw him last. Since John left, Sylvia didn't visit like she did when John was still here. When she visited without John, she would leave Pete and cry for hours because not only did she know that she would miss being with Pete, but she would feel the pain of missing John more than ever. She loved those two guys more than they would ever know.

Peter jumped into Sylvia's arm as she reached the front porch. He was so happy to see her. He told her that he was having a birthday party and asked her if she wanted to come. Sylvia explained to him that she was there for his party, but she came early so that she could help Mrs. Riley set up. Peter ran off to play while the two ladies busied themselves in the kitchen.

Sylvia loved and respected Mrs. Riley for never making her feel like less of a mom to Pete. She was really a true woman of God. She had heard someone say that about Mrs. Kiser once and she almost puked. There was nothing Godly about that woman. Mrs. Riley reminded Sylvia of the Proverbs 31 woman, virtuous. She took care of her husband, Pete, house, wardrobe, and everyone else that needed care. Sylvia wanted to be like her one day if she ever got to leave home.

Peter was so happy to have both of his mommies at his birthday party. Pete and the other children got so dirty playing in the dirt.

They rolled in it, kicked it, and they even ate some of it before the day was through. Sylvia loved the way that Pete was enjoying his childhood.

Sylvia looked at Peter and saw the innocence that he possessed. She then felt a calm spirit run all over her body. She realized that it was God and God alone who had taken Peter out of his hellacious environment and saw fit for him to be raised where he would be protected from all danger, seen and unseen. She realized that the tears that she had cried for several years needed to dry up. Her baby boy wouldn't had stood a chance living under Mr. Kiser's roof, everyone that she knew under Kiser's roof were cursed, cursed by a power much greater than Mr. Kiser himself.

Mrs. Riley called all of the children to the man-made wooden table under the old oak tree outback. Hanging from the tree was a tire swing that Sylvia remembered like yesterday. John had helped Mr. Riley hang that swing the day before he left Deer Island. That was the last thing that he'd done for Peter before he left. Tears welled in Sylvia's eyes as she thought of John and how she wished her family was complete and together. If this war didn't end soon, so that John could return, Sylvia just knew that she would die in war against Kiser. How could she survive something that she knew she could not defeat?

The Riley's had prepared a feast on today. Mr. Riley had killed a small pig and roasted it on open fire. Mrs. Riley had fried up several of their yard chickens. Sylvia wanted to know her secret for getting those yard birds' meat tender enough to fry. Frying yard chicken was something she had never seen Mrs. Kiser do. Mrs. Kiser always stewed her chicken for hours. That was the only way to get it tender enough to swallow down. Sylvia always felt that the yard chicken toughened their meat on purpose right before the kill. She would watch as they ran for their life, but once caught, their necks would be cut or wronged and they would dance all over the yard or fence until the last breath left their bodies. Sylvia felt that chickens knew when their times were drawing near. Mr. Kiser would capture them and pen them up for at least a month and feed them off of corn alone before he killed them. No one wanted to eat a chicken that was still roaming the grounds eating worms, other bugs, or whatever they saw as appetizing. Sylvia thought with this warning, the chickens would toughen their meats hoping that humans would stop seeing them as something tasty and scrumptious. So far, it didn't work. Every black person that Sylvia knew, knew how to make chicken taste so good. The fry chicken that Mrs. Riley cooked today tasted so good that every child asked for more. Mr. Riley explained to Sylvia, "See when I slaughter my chickens I always grabbed them around the neck, pull the neck, and then cut their head off. This allows most of the blood to come out while they dance around headless. See that blood can spoil the meat, make it tougher. And I never kill my old rooster; a man couldn't digest him if they tried. See, your father Mr. Kiser, he always wring his chickens' neck to kill them. The blood can't escape that way, makes the meat tougher. But you know as well as I do, he won't listen to anybody but himself."

Sylvia watched as Peter ate and she counted it as a blessing that God had seen fit to shield her child from the hatred of a Kiser man. From today on Sylvia was going to thank God for his blessing and on those days she remembered crying, there would be no more tears. Instead, Sylvia will smile and rejoice and give God all the praise. This was the first time she recalled herself thinking about

God's grace and mercy. All before she felt like God had left and forsaken her, but right know she felt His love and kindness. Sylvia said to herself, "This is the day that the Lord has made. I will rejoice and be glad in it."

Mrs. Riley bought the cake out and the children all screamed with joy. They all couldn't wait to have a piece of Peter's chocolate birthday cake. Mrs. Riley baked the cake, but she allowed Sylvia to ice the cake. She always wanted Sylvia to feel a part of Peter's upbringing. Mrs. Riley felt as though God as well as Sylvia had given her this opportunity to raise a child that she had tried over and over to be able to do herself, but failed. She wasn't going to let God or Sylvia down. A twelve year-old had done what she couldn't, and that is birth a child. Mrs. Riley counted Peter as a blessing.

The children sung happy birthday to Peter. When it was time for Peter to make a wish, he kept his eyes closed forever. Mrs. Riley asked Peter if he was okay. Peter replied, "I just wished that I could see John today. I miss him so much. So I wished that when I open my eyes that he would be here. I have to keep my eyes closed long enough for him to get here."

"Peter, I told you before, John is away doing something great for our country so that you can have a better place to live. He can't wait to come back home, but he can't come back until his job has finish. John misses you too; remember how much he said that in the last letter he wrote to you. He also told you that when he comes back home, he has the biggest surprise for you," Mrs. Riley explained!

"I know mommy, I know. I'll open my eyes now, it was worth the try. Thank you too, Mommy Sylvia for coming to my party. I missed you too," said Peter.

Sylvia walked home that evening happier than she ever was. Her baby boy Pete was healthy, strong, and happy. She would close her eyes tonight and hear him say, "Mommy Sylvia, Mommy Sylvia, all night long." At that moment, God allowed peace to be still, and Sylvia smiled a great big smile.

Chapter 9

When Sylvia got home that night Mr. Kiser was up to his normal routine, preparing for bed. Lately he was so paranoid before bedtime that he didn't bother her as much. One night Sylvia saw him gathering forks to put under his pillow, tonight he was loading his gun. Sylvia had seen this fool sleep with this shotgun loaded over his bed many nights. Tonight he also had a broom. She never saw Mr. Kiser taking the broom to bed. So she asked, "Is there something you would like for me to sweep up for you?"

"Did I tell you to sweep something, or are you just being noisy?"

"I'm sorry, just wanted to help if I could."

"You better go on and mind your business before I ask you to do something else!"

Sylvia rushed off to get ready for bed. She really didn't care why he was going to bed with all of that stuff. She hoped that the stuff he carried to the room with him would enjoy being in there with him more than she did. She wondered how Mrs. Kiser could sleep next to this mad man while he had a loaded gun above their bed and forks underneath his pillow. For now, only God knew what he was going to do with the broom. To her surprise, Mr. Kiser didn't have

49

the old worn broom that they were told to sweep with; he carried the new full broom that had never swept a floor.

Mr. Kiser didn't tell anyone why he started carrying these odd things to bed with him every night. He had never remembered fearing anything since he reached adulthood except for now. In the past month, Mr. Kiser had experienced something he'd only heard old people talk about. At night once he was fast asleep, someone would pay him a visit. He had first had the visit while both his wife Mary and Sylvia were asleep in the bed with him. He didn't see it, but it got on him and rode him for miles. It felt like it sucked his blood, suffocated him and stole his breath. He couldn't move or say a word. He could feel Sylvia's body against his and he knew that Mary was right next to Sylvia, but as much as he tried, he couldn't mutter a single word. One night this thing tried to ride him so hard, Mr. Kiser thought that he was going to die right there. He knew that he was awake because the thought of dying with dirty underwear on was killing him even more. Why hadn't he washed his stank tail and changed his underwear he thought. "I don't want to die this way!" He tried screaming, but nothing would come out. He tried to move and couldn't move. This thing was heavy and wild. At one point, Kiser thought that he was free. He felt himself running out of the bed to get Joseph so that he could help him find this thing and kill it, but as soon as he thought he was free, this thing pulled him back on the bed, held him down, like it was teasing him. It bounced on top of him again, riding him for miles. When it released Kiser this time, he slapped his face to make sure that he was awake and free. He looked over at both ladies sleeping beside him and couldn't believe that they slept and didn't see or hear anything. He was so afraid, he didn't even want to walk pass a mirror. "What in the hell was that?"

Mr. Kiser laid back down and thought about all of the evil stories that he'd heard years ago. The older people would always speak of hags and their evil doings. They would say that hags only paid you visits at night while you were sleeping. Mr. Kiser couldn't understand why a hag would want to ride him of all people; he had never bothered a soul. After getting a visit several times, Mr. Kiser tried to remember what the people had said about stopping the old hag from coming by. The first that he remembered was placing a fork under his pillow; the hag was supposed to sense this protection. That didn't work. Then Mr. Kiser had remembered what old Mr. Smith had said about the loaded gun over his bed keeping the hag away from him. Mr. Smith had said that the hag didn't like gun powder and could smell it a mile away. The loaded gun over Kiser's bed didn't work either. The first night that the hag came in and Kiser had the gun over his bed, he was on my back, arms down my side and he heard the footsteps coming towards his bed, along with a very graphical character of an old shaggy man. It slowly hopped onto his chest while smiling demonically, with one hand it began to choke Kiser, while it then closed in on his face and laughed right into Mr. Kiser's face. It felt like the old hag grabbed a hold of the gun while riding Mr. Kiser and this forced more pressure on top of him. When it jumped off of Kiser, Mr. Kiser tried to look up quickly to see what this thing look like or who it was. When Kiser gained full use of his body it was then that he saw the creature slipping out of his bedroom window. Could it be who he thought it was? It looked like the back of his head and the small of his back. But it couldn't be, it couldn't be Mr. Old Tyson. He had heard that if a hag came and paid you a visit, it was someone old that you knew. They said that the old person lived longer by robbing younger people of their blood at night. One man had told Kiser that if you see the old person the day after the hag paid you a visit, if it was that person who rode you, he couldn't look you in the eye. Mr. Kiser was terrified. "Why would Mr. Tyson's old soul want to leave his body at night and come ride me?"

On this particular night, when Sylvia had seen him, Mr. Kiser was scared to go to bed. His body still felt exhausted from the hag ride the night before. There was something else that Kiser remembered right before Sylvia came into the house, and this was putting a broom across your threshold. The hag was known to sit there and count every straw before entering the person's room which tired the hag out and they would leave without coming in. So, tonight, Mr. Kiser had his loaded gun, forks, and broom. Mr. Kiser without thinking about it, also said something aloud that he had never heard himself say, "Lord, please don't let the hag ride me tonight!" With that, Mr. Kiser laid down next to Mrs. Kiser and went to sleep. He awoke the next morning and almost jumped for joy. "You old hag, you knew better than to mess with Mr. Kiser last night." Kiser then put all of his hag prevention things away because the last thing that he wanted was for anyone to find out that anything had ever bothered or frightened Mr. Big Bad Kiser.

Mrs. Kiser had breakfast waiting when Mr. Kiser walked into the small kitchen the next morning. "Good Morning Kiser, how did you sleep?"

"Why the hell you ask me something stupid like that for? I always sleep well when I lay down in my bed at night! Tell me why you asked that woman!"

"I was just asking. Please sit down and eat your grits, eggs, sausage, and bacon. That meat that you cured last time sure turned out great. Whatever you did to it, you need to do it that way all of the time. Just wait until you taste the sausage."

"I really don't think I want to eat any of it. You do know that's my old sow that died from bringing her litter. I didn't want to waste all of that meat so I figured it was best to turn her into bacon and sausage. She was a big heifer! She was good to me for a lot of years. I believe I got over three-hundred pigs from that one sow. I didn't save her head for hog head cheese like I did the other hogs that I slaughtered, cause she died fighting a good fight. It felt as though she died for me, so that I could have more. Hours after Joseph had helped her bring her piglets she passed away. I believe that it was all of the blood loss and her old age that did her in. It was like her body started shutting down during the whole process and she couldn't push any more. Didn't for Joseph I would have lost all of my piglets too. I buried her head near the corn field, I felt like she would be happier there. That hog loved to eat."

"Oh my God, Kiser, I've been pinching off this meat all morning and had no clue that it was the old sow. I think that I'm going to throw up. I remembered that day when I was outback hanging clothes on the line. I reached down to pick up another piece and caught her coming from the side of my eyes. She could have rammed right into me, but instead she just ran beside me knocking me off of my feet. She circled back around and looked at me lying helplessly on the ground. That's when I saw three of her piglets dashed from near the clothes line. I realized then that she felt as though I was a danger to her babies. I laid right there for awhile being as still as I knew how until the sow had gathered her piglets and left out of sight. Oh, how I thanked God that morning. She could have hurt me, but she meant no harm if need be. From that day on I respected her. If she was out of the pen roaming the grounds, I would get out of her way. It didn't matter what I was doing. One day while walking to the old outhouse to take a dump, I saw her and her piglets and decided the near woods were a better choice. That was my first and only time wiping my butt with moss. I can't eat any more of this meat. You just spoiled it for me."

Paul listened from his room as his father recalled the events of that night the sow died and couldn't help but to visualized all the facts that his dad did leave out. Why didn't he tell his mom how he raped him right there in the barn while the poor sow suffered. He was getting sick just remembering for himself. He cried like it was the night of the brutal attack. Oh, how he hurt. Paul's heart had ached way more than his butt. Every time that he pictured it, Paul always tried to picture the man ramming from behind as a stranger and not the man that was suppose to love, protect, and shelter him. Oh, how could a man do this to his own flesh and blood and act like nothing had ever happened. Right now Paul was still in his room because his dad was near. Since that night, Paul tried to avoid contact as much as he could. He now saw his father as an animal, once bitten, you learn to stay away.

"Those boys better show themselves before I have to go and look for them. They better get up before I get them up! They could've been married and out my house already, sorry punks!"

"Kiser, Paul should be coming out soon. I heard him up in his room hours ago. Joseph, he was gone before I got up this morning. You know that he takes right after you, don't want the sun to catch him still buried under the covers."

Mr. Kiser took another drink of water before getting up from the table and nearly choked. He coughed until his eyes watered. Mrs. Kiser quickly ran over to him and started beating him on the back. After Mr. Kiser stopped coughing, he pulled away from his wife. "Get off of me woman! I don't need your help. Water just went down the wrong pipe, that's all. You think that I'm weak like that son of yours in there or something. He can't even get his feet wet before he's sick and crawling under your breast. I'm going on out. You better get him out of this house today and make him do something. Tell him to pick up the eggs so that Joseph can help me over in the north field. I don't want to hear any excuses about him helping with Sarah when I get back!"

"Kiser, don't worry, I'll take care of Paul. I will tell him as you said. He'll get the eggs, that's no problem. Do you want him to come over to the north field when he's done?"

"No, keep the chick near the nest near you; don't want him to feel out of place with the real Kiser men!"

Hearing his dad put him down and show his love for Joseph more than he loved him was really getting to Paul. He couldn't even begin to imagine how his sister Sarah felt not being able to express herself at all and living alone in such a dark quiet room. After he heard his father leave, he yelled out, "Why couldn't he just choke and die?" He then went into Sarah's room to bathe her. While he bathed her fragile body, he sung to her. Paul told her that one day she would be able to sit outside in the sunlight and see the beauty of the earth. No man shall hold you in bondage forever, no man! He went into the kitchen and got the plate that his mom had made for Sarah and made sure that she ate it. He hated how his mother would open Sarah's door and slide her plate in there like she was an unwanted orphan. How could a mother treat her own baby that way just to satisfy such a hateful man, Paul didn't understand. After he emptied Sarah's bucket, he lifted her up to the window so that she could be face to face with the sun. He knew that Sarah would be alone for at least another twelve hours once he left her.

After hearing about the old sow this morning, Paul took a few slice of bread and passed on the rest of the breakfast. He was headed out of the back door when he heard the front door shut quietly. He snuck back down the hall to see whom was sneaking in. He heard the steps but they were moving fast. He knew that one set of footsteps was his mother's because she always drug her feet, but who owned the other set of footsteps? It definitely wasn't Joseph or his dad. Paul had to get a closer look. He couldn't understand why they weren't in the den or kitchen. As he got closer to his parents room, Paul heard a voice that he was so familiar with. Why did it sound like the sermon he heard on Sunday mornings? The only difference was, instead of the voice saying, "Fix it Jesus fix it!" The voice was saying, "Mary, Mary fix it, put that Holy Ghost on me Mary! Make me shout girl!" Paul knew that he couldn't open the door, but he wanted to, he needed to see this for himself. He wanted to see the man who was bold enough to come into his father's house and take something that Kiser thought was his. Paul opened the door and Pastor Baker said, "Hallelujah, I have sinned, please son forgive me!"

Paul looked at his mother, "I'm sorry, I came to ask my mom what was I suppose to do today. I didn't realize that you had a visitor. But while I'm here, let me ask you one thing. Is this all you can say for yourself? You'd rather give yourself to another man than show your own children the love that a mother has for her children." Paul didn't wait for a response because he knew that he wasn't suppose to see what he had just seen. Mrs. Kiser thought that Paul was long gone when she let the Pastor in. She didn't realize that he had spent extra time with Sarah on this morning. She was now praying that Paul would keep his mouth shut. At the same time she was trying to get Pastor Baker out of the house making sure that they were facing the complete opposite of the north field. Mrs. Kiser was thanking God that once her husband went into the fields during the day; he stayed for long hours getting lost out there until his work was done.

Pastor Baker was back at the church by now praying for somebody else while thanking God for saving him an hour ago. His congregation worshipped him sometimes more than they worshipped God and Pastor Baker knew that. He asked the Lord for forgiveness and repented for the tenth time that week. Boy did the women of Deer Island Baptist keep him prayed up and satisfied. If he kept this up, Pastor Baker knew that one day he'd have to prepare for his own funeral. And not even the hardest preaching, praying, singing, best dressing and smelling Pastor knew how he could do that.

Chapter 10

Paul ran and ran until he reached the spot in the woods where his father's moonshine still was. "Sylvia, Sylvia, where are you?"

"What's wrong, you never come back here? Did something happen to Sarah? Is she okay?"

"Sarah is fine. Why would you think that something was wrong with Sarah?"

"Well, I know that's where you have been all morning, unless this morning was somewhat different, and that would be unusual."

"Well, you're right. I did take care of Sarah for most of the morning. That reminds me of something I've been thinking about asking you for awhile. Before I ask, please tell me why you're up in that tree?"

"I can see Deer Island from up here. It also protects me from some of the wild animals that roam this part of the forest." Sylvia didn't want to tell Paul that she had been climbing this tree for years because of her fear of Mr. Kiser. That day when Mr. Kiser snuck up on her and raped her flashes upon her every time that she enters the forest. "So what do you want to ask me?"

"Please don't mention this too anyone. I'm planning to leave Deer Island. I want to go as far north as my saved money can take me. The only thing, I mean person that is holding me back is Sarah. See, I know that you can take care of yourself, but how long would Sarah live without me being here to watch after her. I've cried so many nights behind this, knowing that I could've been long gone out of this Hell Hole of a place called home. If only I could pack her away in a suitcase and take her with me. I've said time and time again, if Sarah and I walked off of Kiser's farm tomorrow, no one would come looking for us. Mom and dad cares nothing about us. If only I knew where I was going and what I would be doing, I would at least try and take her with me, but for now, Sarah is better off in her dark cell than walking the dangerous streets with me."

"So, how much have you really thought about this move?"

"I've been thinking about it since I finished high school. At that time, I didn't have a dime to my name, but since then, I've saved every penny mom have given me for helping out with her duties. You know how lazy she can be, she loves it when I carry the house for her. Only if Dad knew how much I cooked and cleaned he wouldn't see me as helpless. But Mom wants to keep all of my good deeds a secret so that she can get the credit for it. Please don't get mad when I tell you this Sylvia. You know all of those times that you have accused Joseph of stealing Kiser's shine, well he is not your thief, I am. I picked up a few customers along the way and I have been selling my shine for a little cheaper than Dad sells his. I'm sorry for all of the bad blood that I have caused you and Joseph, but I had to get this money. I didn't see any other way. Please forgive me."

"I'll forgive you alright. I'm in this woods sun up to sun down, hot or cold, no help from anyone and now you want my forgiveness. I do understand you wanting to get away from here, but did you ever think about including me in your little escape plan. Do you think that you are the only one that Mr. Kiser hates? Do you feel like just as long as you know that someone is taking care of Sarah that you could live happy ever after and forget those that just couldn't get away? Paul, are you just that selfish? Just to think that I was about to jump out of this tree to be eye-to-eye with you, you are no different from the other animals I seek protection from."

"Sylvia, I'm sorry that you feel this way. This is why it took me so long to talk to you about this. I feel your hurt. I've looked at you for years and envied you. I would always ask the Lord why out of all of Kiser's kids that he had to make you the most perfect. You have beauty, brains, and so far, I've found no flaws. It seems as though God made sure that something was wrong with me, Joseph, and Sarah that people would instantly take notice of with the naked eye. When you were younger, I use to hate you for being perfect. I treated you the way that I did because if I could be you, I would trade places in an instant. But something happen one day that made me realize that there shouldn't be a reason in this world why any man should want to do harm to another the way harm has been done to us, especially when the person that harms you is your own flesh and blood."

"Paul, did something happen to you?"

"Sylvia, you have the prettiest eyes, highest cheekbones, and the fullest lips. Your skin is as golden as honey and your hair is as soft as cotton. This morning God decided to free me. I have believed within my heart for so long that God just hated us and loved you in a special way. I saw how Dad showed his hate for you during the day, but at night, he would beckon you to come sleep with him and momma. I would tell myself that he was doing what he could to hold on to you since you were his youngest and that you were like the only girl he had since he treated Sarah like a prisoner. Through all of those beliefs, God saw fit to answer my prayer."

"How did he do that Paul?"

"Before leaving the house this morning, I just so happened to be called to momma's room by an unseen power. Something was telling me to knock and the door shall be open, but instead of knocking I opened the door by faith. When I opened the door and looked in, I couldn't believe it."

"Believe what?"

"Even though you were outside, back here in these woods, I opened the door and looked into your eyes. I saw your high cheek-bones and full lips. Instead of skin as golden as honey, I saw skin so bright that it was yellow."

"Paul, I don't get any of this. What are you saying? How could you see my eyes, lips, and cheekbones if you didn't see me?"

"Sylvia, I have always wondered why you were so different from the rest of us. Today God revealed to me why after all these years of me asking him. I don't know how to tell you this or if I should tell you."

"Hey, you told me this much, you better tell me or I'm killing you right here today and you can kiss your little plan of escape goodbye."

"Okay, I'll tell you, but promise to keep this between you and me. Don't go around asking questions or that will get you or both of us killed! Now listen and listen closely because I will only say this one time. Mr. Kiser is not your father!"

"Oh, really and you're just now figuring that one out!"

"So you knew, all along?"

"I knew that much just by observation and listening to my mother's prayers when I was a little girl. What I don't know is who my father is?"

"That's how I figured it out Sylvia. When I opened the door today, Pastor Baker was in momma's room banging momma. When I say banging momma, he was banging momma so hard, that the headboard was speaking in tongues."

"Pastor Baker, you mean our Deer Island Baptist Church, Pastor Baker? He was in momma's room in Mr. Kiser's bed?"

"Yes, the one and only Pastor Baker. Picture him Sylvia; think about his eyes, his whole face. It's yours, except for your darker skin complexion. But you are what you get when you mix yellow and black."

"You mean to tell me that I have to live and sleep with the Devil and the man's seed that created me is that close to God!

This is unbelievable! There's no way that he knows, not the way he looks over me when I've seen him. This man has never spoken to me directly. Could this be the reason why Mother stopped me from going to church, because she was afraid of someone seeing the resemblance? She told me that I couldn't go back to church because I got pregnant at a young age and the church folks saw that as a sin so big that I couldn't go back until I was called. I asked her one day when I really wanted to go cause I was feeling really, really, bad; 'Momma who is going to call me?' The woman told me that God himself had to call me! No wonder that She-Devil stays up in the church. Her and Kiser deserves each other! I am fuming mad. Let me get out of this tree before someone sees smoke and comes running back here."

"You are so right Sylvia. When I was younger, I thought that Daddy was the worse person that walked this earth, but now that I'm older; I don't know who would get out of the sack first if someone put momma and daddy in a sack together. I think that all of Kiser's hatred rubbed off on her and she forgot how to love. She forgot how to love her own children, but from what I saw today with my own two eyes, it looks like she remembered how to love Pastor Baker!"

"Paul, you keep mentioning your Dad's hatred and you said earlier about us being harmed by our own flesh and blood. What happened to you? I didn't realize that you were hurting so much. Looking at you from the outside, I would never see that something has been bothering you enough to make you just want to leave your family."

"I've been through a lot of pain living her in Deer Island. I've had my share of life here on the farm. I promised to carry all of my hurt to the grave."

"If I share, will you share?"

"Maybe."

"Well, you better listen up and you better listen up closely. I'm going to make a long story short. When I've said all that I've had to say, don't feel sorry for me. I want you to leave Deer Island just like you've been dreaming of. I'll take care of my sister. I probably won't be able to stay in her room as long as you do, but I can promise you that she'll get at least two meals a day, washed up, and I'll empty her bucket."

"You won't have time for all of that. Dad said long time ago that your place is back here in these woods. You make him rich. He'd be a poor man just like these other black farmers if he didn't have your famous shine."

"Don't worry about me making Kiser's shine. You just worry about getting out of here. Now listen up. I'm going to tell you the real reason that I go up in that tree. On my sixteenth birthday, our dear mother gave me, her bastard daughter to her husband. She couldn't tell me herself so she got herself lost that day allowing Kiser to have his way with me. He snuck up on me right here at the still. You remember that day when you took care of my burned feet. Well Kiser caught me on the ground that day shortly after my foot was burned. He raped me and told me that from that day on, I was his. It was the first day that he ever showed any type ownership of me."

"I'm so sorry Sylvia!"

"Those nights when you were feeling jealous of me because you saw your Dad beckon for me to come into his bedroom, I was wishing that I could be you. Every time that you saw me go in there, he got on top of me and did his business. Oh, how did it hurt for Mr. Kiser to be on top of me while my mother lied right there beside me with our hips touching. Can you believe that one night while I was crying, this sick lady reached over and touched me and told me that it was going to be alright? I've been through the storm more than once or twice. I've been living in this storm forever."

"Sylvia, you have to come with me! No child should have to endure what we have endured right here amongst our own."

"You still haven't told me what happened to you."

"Sylvia, just like you, I was raped by Kiser. He claimed that he raped me for being a sissy." Paul told Sylvia all about the first time in the barn that night when they were trying to help the sow. He went on to tell her that Kiser had done it again on four separate occasions."

"Oh, no Paul! Mr. Kiser is worse off than I thought. I figured that he thought all along that it was okay to have sex with me because I wasn't his child and deep down he'd known that since the day that I was born, but for Kiser to rape and have sex with his own flesh and blood, his first born son, how sick? Paul, please leave this place as soon as you can. Let me know what I can do to help get you out of here."

"We both have to leave here. Let's leave here together."

"No, I'll stay and look after Sarah. You go and prepare a place for us. I only ask that you don't leave and forget about us here still under Kiser's abuse.

"I won't forget about my only two sisters. I love you guys."

Chapter 11

Oh my God, how am I going to get this dog off of me! I can't yell for help and this bitch won't let me go! Lord, help!

Joseph had left the house before sun up this morning, hoping to get his needs met. He had been awoken by his hardness and just the touch of his covers made him quiver. The rain had fallen the night before which placed Joseph in a deep sleep. He remembered dreaming of the most beautiful woman he knew, Sylvia. He didn't understand why Satan wanted to be so cruel to him. Of all the woman in Deer Island, why would Satan choose Sylvia for Joseph's fantasies? This had happened many times before and Joseph was getting sick of it. "She is my damn sister, I'm not that screwed up!"

Joseph got dressed and ran out of the house before anyone could hear him and ask about his goings. The air was still and the land was quiet. Joseph thought that his way was clear until something heavy landed on his left foot. Joseph was scared to look down because of the warm, wet, slimy matter that had just pounced on him. Whatever it was, it sure wasn't trying to get off. Joseph walked more into the moon light so that he could identify this courageous creature. It appeared to be glued to Joseph's shoe, because as Joseph walked he kicked and it didn't fly off. When Joseph finally found some natural light, he looked down at his

69

foot. Glaring into his eyes were two large terrified eyes. Sitting on top of Joseph's boot was the biggest pond chicken Joseph had ever seen. "Wow!"

If Joseph wasn't so serious about his mission, killing this toad would be a real treat for his father. His Dad had referred to these large toads as pond chickens every since Joseph could remember. He said that he called them that because they lived in the pond and tasted like chicken. As Joseph watched it slowly try to make its way off of his boot, Joseph figured that this one was probably the size of a full grown chicken too. He had never seen such a creature. "What a trophy?"

Joseph remembered that the sun would soon be up if he didn't continue on his way. Why did he have to go so far? He asked himself this, but he already knew the answer. The first time that Joseph did this was several years ago. Joseph had experienced a sensation that he had never experience before in his life until the night he put his hand so far up a hog's vagina that he brought forth all of her babies. He had wet on himself and it felt great. Joseph tossed and turned for a couple of months thinking about that feeling. He would wake up many mornings with his hardness in his hands, but it didn't matter how long or hard he stroked himself that feeling would not return.

One day while out doing his chores, Joseph heard what sounded like pigs fighting. He snuck around the wooded side of the pen and hid behind a tree. He saw one of Kiser's boars running behind a sow with a little pink drill hanging from beneath him. The boar mounted the sow a few times, but each time the sow would run alongside the pen forcing the boar off of her back. Joseph watched this same act repeatedly while waiting anxiously for the boar to enter the sow. When it looked as though the boar was about to give up, Joseph ran and threw some fresh corn and slop in the far side of the pen. The large boar noticed this and ran over there to be the first at the trough. Joseph hurriedly closed the boar off from the other side of the pen. Joseph then threw in some corn and slop for the sow. This was a very young and small sow. Joseph had heard his dad tell one of his helpers a few days ago that this sow didn't know what was going on, she was very young and had never mated before. She was afraid of the boar and the boar was probably too large for her any way. Kiser had said if anything didn't happen in a week, he was going to swap out the boar for a smaller boar. Kiser fastened those two up together because he knew that this boar out of all of his boars, knew how to handle business. But would he be able to handle business if his load was too heavy for the poor small sow to carry?

Joseph was still aroused as he watched the sow from behind as she stuck her head down into the trough trying to devour everything in sight. Her cute little curled tailed, twitched every so often as she enjoyed the meal given to her. Joseph had come prepared to go to work, he remembered how the large sow kicked while he pulled out her pigs, so he knew the strength of those hind legs. Joseph snuck behind the sow. She didn't move because she was so use to his presence, she trusted him. Joseph quickly grabbed the sow by her back legs and binded them tightly together. He pulled down his pants and got behind her and entered her gently like the big boar couldn't. He had been waiting on this day for a long time. He had wondered how it would feel to have his penis inside of the sow that night. Joseph had figured if having his hands in her felt that good, putting his man parts in had to take him to the moon and back. So, after going to the moon that day and coming back, Joseph knew that this wouldn't be his last trip.

Dinner seemed to last for hours that night once everyone had returned to the house for the evening. Joseph felt sweat gleaming on his face as Kiser asked him so many questions about today's events. Mr. Kiser wanted to know why Joseph had separated the boar and the sow. He also wanted to know why Joseph had feed them the slop that was meant for the next day feeding, knowing that Joseph had fed them earlier that evening. For Mr. Kiser, none of it made sense, especially coming from Joseph. Mr. Kiser felt like Joseph could run his farm in the same manner as him if something should happen to him tomorrow.

Joseph had goofed and let his feelings get the best of him. After getting off of the sow, he did untie her and set her free. He was thanking God that he remembered to do that. Joseph hadn't even thought about opening the dividing gate back so that the sow and boar would be in the same pen again. He couldn't believe that he had been so stupid. So much for going to bed on cloud nine tonight thought Joseph. Even though he had answered all of Kiser's questions, he still knew in the back of Mr. Kiser's head he was wondering what really happened at the hog pen that day. Kiser's questions didn't stop Joseph cold turkey that day. He was feeling emotions that he had never felt before in his life. The sow didn't even fight him anymore. It was almost as if she wanted Joseph as much as Joseph wanted her. At least, this is what Joseph was beginning to assume. Joseph did this several times until one day he almost got caught.

Joseph had never heard of anyone else wanting to do this with animals. He knew this was weird, but to ease his mind a little, he would always say, "Well at least it's better than doing it to my own sister."

So on tonight, Joseph had another plan of satisfying his needs. A few days ago, an old dog had wandered on their farm. Joseph had planned this thing out carefully, because it had been a while since he had satisfied himself. He knew that he couldn't risk getting caught with one of his dad's pigs. He had heard Pastor Baker's sermon a few months ago, "Warning comes before destruction." So after planning carefully, Joseph made his crate way back there on the other side of the north field. No one came back here as much as he did. Joseph fed the dog several days back there trying to gain his loyalty. He kept the dog in the crate while he was away. The dog finally began to walk up to him, licked his hands and beckoned to his call, so Joseph felt like it was time.

Joseph knew that he needed to hurry, because sometimes his dad got an early start as well. When Joseph finally reached the crate, he opened it and let out his friend. Joseph then pulled out his pork chop from last night's dinner and threw it down to the dog. While the dog was busy tackling the bone from the pork chop, Joseph pulled down his pants and entered her. He knew that she was in heat from the first day that he saw her. Ooh, did Joseph think this was better than being behind a fat hog.

Joseph tried to thrust like he'd imagined doing since he planned this. He had no problems moving in and out of the sow, but for some reason, Joseph could not move. He pushed against the dog. Joseph clawed the dog, but nothing would give. Joseph was stuck tight into this dog's tight vagina. It was now to the point that it appeared the dog really wanted Joseph off of her too. She was doing all that she could to drag Joseph off. Joseph was hurting bad, several times he thought that he would faint. He kept hoping that the dog would loosen its grip.

Hours had gone by and Joseph and the dog were still stuck together. Joseph knew for show that his penis was going to fall off as soon as it came out. Joseph had picked up a piece of stick as the dog was dragging him and hit her with it, but all of the beating still didn't free him. The worst part of this was that the sun had been out for a long time now and he heard Mr. Kiser's footsteps coming. His dad sounded mad as he called Joseph's name. Joseph didn't dare answer, instead he prayed to God asking him to not let his dad find him like this. Joseph was so weak that he couldn't fight any longer.

Just as Mr. Kiser walked up on the scene, he saw something that day that made him have a bowel movement in his pants. "Joseph, Joseph, Joseph, what are you doing son? Get the hell up from there!"

"Dad, I can't, but I can explain. It's not what it looks like."

"You have your stuff in a bitch or whatever you want to call it. That's what it looks like to me from here! Tell me what it looks like from where you are?"

"Dad, I'm stuck, please help me before someone sees me like this!"

Mr. Kiser tried all that he could to free his boy, but Joseph wasn't budging. He picked up the hugest branch that he could find and Kiser beat the dog so much that he was about to kill Joseph. Mr. Kiser had no choice than to holler for help because it looked like Joseph was about to turn blue. After some calling, Sylvia and Paul came running up on the scene. The three of them pulled and pulled and finally Joseph was free from the bitch. No one would ever forget what they saw that day.

Chapter 12

Joseph was going to die. Sylvia didn't know when but she was in mourning for his poor soul already while it was yet alive. Kiser had beaten him so bad. Sylvia didn't know where Joseph was, but she did find one of his front teeth by the cinder block back steps. She had prayed for her brother the whole time her and Paul carried him back to the house. She didn't know what the dog had done to him that made him unable to walk. Seeing her brother stuck to a dog was nerve racking and nauseating. Sylvia's stomach was turning just picturing what she had seen. As she followed Joseph's blood, she hoped that he was still alive. Sylvia got frightened when the blood trail had ended and there was still no sign of Joseph.

The one book that Kiser had never taken from Sylvia was the Bible. She spent most of her waking hours reading the Bible and studying it as she tended the still. There were several verses in the Bible that came to mind as Sylvia thought about what Joseph had done. In Exodus 22 Sylvia recalled it saying, "Whoever lies with an animal shall surely be put to death." And in the book of Deuteronomy it said, "Cursed is he who lies with any animal." Sylvia needed her brother to live. The thought of anyone dying by the hands of Mr. Kiser had haunted Sylvia for a long time. For him to kill his flesh and blood she couldn't imagine before tonight, but after

Paul had shared how Kiser raped him so brutally, Sylvia knew that there was a chance that Mr. Kiser could kill her brother. The wages for this type of sin was death. The Bible spoke of it. Sylvia so needed to find her brother and make him repent before it was too late for his soul. Sylvia wondered how far Mr. Kiser would drag Joseph after such terrible beating. She didn't want to call for him because she was uncertain if Mr. Kiser was still out there in the wilderness with them. Sylvia realized that it was best for her to go back to the house, because if she ran into Mr. Kiser she was very certain that she would have gotten beaten next. She had promised John that she would stay out of harm's way if not for herself she would for a future with him and Peter.

When Sylvia walked into the house, she saw Mary in the kitchen. She asked her mom, "Have you seen Joseph?"

"No I haven't, he left out before we woke up this morning. Kiser came in here a few minutes ago and told me that he had found him and he was up to no good. Was he caught stealing Kiser's moonshine red-handed this time?"

"Moon shine, he wasn't caught stealing no moonshine. This is so much bigger than moonshine! You mean to tell me that you didn't even ask Mr. Kiser what was going on. What kind of mother are you? Do you want to sit in this house and see all of your kids suffer under the hands of a man that you don't even love your damn self?"

Mrs. Kiser stretched out her hand and smacked Sylvia on her left cheek. Sylvia turned her other cheek and said, "Go ahead, slap the right cheek while you are at it."

Mrs. Kiser burst out crying. There was no one to console her. Sylvia allowed her to sob until she fell to the floor. Sylvia looked down on her and asked her mother, "Is Pastor Baker my father? Be honest with me mother!"

Mrs. Kiser never responded to Sylvia's question that day. She lied there lifeless, too embarrassed to reveal her face. She wanted so bad to turn things around, but as a mother of four kids and a wife to Mr. George Kiser, Mary just didn't know how to do it. She only knew what to do to survive. She had heard her mother tell her almost every day as a child, "You better do whatever it takes you to live, don't worry about anyone else. It's every man for themselves." Her mother would tell them this and leave them without the tiniest morsel of their next meal. Mary Kiser had always lived by the motto: "Survival of the fittest!"

Sylvia left her mom on the floor that day and went into a closet to pray. Before she began praying, Sylvia asked the Lord something she had asked him time and time again, "Why would you allow a hateful man like Kiser to marry a Mary and become a father to children given names; Paul, Joseph, and Sarah?" These were all strong Biblical names and she had heard that Mr. George Kiser named all of Mary's offspring including her. Why did Kiser name me Sylvia, of all names? Sylvia thought about Joseph, and then thought about Paul. Sylvia thought about Sarah, even thought about her mother who still could be heard sniffling sounding like she was a mile away.

Sylvia prayed: "Oh Heavenly Father, I come as humble as I know how. Lord help us in our time of need. Help us Lord. I've looked for Joseph, but I could not find him. I know that You know his whereabouts. God, I'm asking you to protect and comfort him. Joseph is lost and he needs some direction Father. I'm asking you to look upon Him, Jesus and see pass all of His faults. I'm praying for second chances. I'm praying for forgiveness of sins. In spite of weakness, falls, and shortcomings of every kind, Jesus, help Joseph and never forsake him. Heal his broken body, have pity on him, Jesus. I'm asking you to show your perfect love and rescue your dear Joseph. Jesus, I'm calling on your name. Don't forget about Paul. Don't forget about Sarah. Jesus, remember my mother and do not forget about Mr. Kiser. And Lord, if you have just a little blessing left after you have done all of that, I am asking you, please remember me. AMEN!"

"What are you doing in there?" yelled Mr. Kiser.

"I was looking for that order that you gave me. I misplaced it and was hoping that it fell out of my coat pocket. I was down there on the floor looking, Sir."

"Which order, the King Street order?"

"Yes, that's it. I couldn't remember exactly how many cases of shine they wanted. I've made more than enough, but I don't want to bottle up too many. You know we can't give good liquor away."

"That's for sure, so find that order!"

Sylvia knew her orders backwards and forward. She thought Mr. Kiser knew that about her, but today she had to have an answer and that's what she said. She hurried behind Mr. Kiser but not following too closely, she felt like this was her only chance of finding out Joseph whereabouts. Mr. Kiser was headed to the hogs. She hid behind a tree as Kiser went into the pen. It was so hard for Sylvia to see but she did glimpse movement. She then heard Mr. Kiser speak.

"Of all those women out there, why you want to be with a dog? Why the hell would you want to do a dog, Joseph? Do you know why I brought you back here? That sow just had her litter of pigs last night. I threw your bloody behind right beside her and her younglings and she didn't eat your behind up. The sow got up and left her babies and came and snuggled with your nasty ass. I knew something was wrong months ago when you started feeding those hogs more than we ever did before. And that day I found the boar locked up in the other side of the pen, I asked you about that. I guess that you thought I was stupid or something. How long were you having sex with my sow, Joseph?"

Joseph couldn't speak. His lips were swollen and busted and both eyes were sealed shut. He lied there wanting to die. If he could mumble something, it would be, "Kill me now!" Joseph wanted to be free. He wanted to be freed from what he had become and he didn't want anyone to know what he had done. In order for this to happen, he himself knew that he had to die. There was no way he could live here on earth and face the people that caught him in such horrific act on a day-to-day basis. "What have I done?" thought Joseph.

Joseph prayed to the Lord without mumbling a single word: "O God, look down upon me a miserable sinner. Have mercy upon me and deliver me from the trouble that besets me, for which I know I am deservedly suffering. Holy guardian and protector of my soul and body, forgive me every transgression which I have committed

81

this day. God, Lord of life and death let me die now for You know my heart. I cannot bear this burden no more. I ask that You find it somewhere in your heart to forgive me Father. Look after my family, especially my daddy, Lord. For my dad has loved me, loved me more than he loved the others. Only you can command death, God. Please send your Death Angels to see about me. AMEN!"

Mr. Kiser kicked Joseph again in his ribs. "Answer me boy."

Joseph thought, "Couldn't daddy see that I was dying? What more did he want? I had just asked the Lord to take me, and I was waiting, waiting on my Lord, Savior, God, Jesus, Christ. Take me Lord, take me!"

Sylvia watched everything knowing that she had placed Joseph in Jesus' hands and that was all that she could do. She watched as Mr. Kiser covered Joseph still body with a croaker sack and left him against the trough. Sylvia waited for at least ten minutes after Kiser had left before running over to the pen. Joseph's body looked lifeless as she looked down upon him. "Why, Lord why?"

Sylvia hadn't noticed the sow or her piglets lying nearby. She wasn't familiar with her surrounding since most of her time was spent at the still. The sow got up so quickly, there was nothing Sylvia could do. The next thing she knew, Joseph had grabbed her and wrapped his body around hers. Joseph wasn't dead, he was still alive. "Thanks Joseph, you saved me."

Chapter 13

Sylvia was awaken by a kiss. "Sylvia, I must leave now. I will miss you, Sarah, and Joseph a lot, but please do remember that I'm leaving in hopes to find someplace better for all of us. I know that you will watch over Sarah. I will find a way to let you know that I'm okay. I never thought I would say these words, but I love you. Make sure that Sarah knows that I didn't mean to hurt her. When she cries for me, sing 'Yes, Jesus loves me' softly in her left ear while rocking her in your arms. She likes that. If she doesn't stop crying, squeeze her tight against you making sure that she can feel your heartbeat and hold her there until she is comforted. I better go. I wanted to be at least a couple of miles away before the sun peeked its face."

"I'm going to miss you. Take care of yourself and promise me one thing. If you find it harder out there than its here, please come back home. Don't stay away from your family and suffer for your pride. Do find a way to let me know that you are safe."

"I got ya, sis. Keep an eye on Joseph too because he still hurts pretty badly. I'm just glad that Kiser allowed him back in the house. Well, see ya. Remember, you don't know where I am or what I am doing. Thank you, I owe you so much." Paul went into his room where Joseph was still sound asleep. He reached and grabbed his

83

old tore up bible. Paul turned to the twenty-third Psalms where he had hid his money with hopes that the Lord would watch over it. Paul had stashed away six-hundred dollars and felt like this amount for a decent amount to get him away from here.

As Paul lowered himself out the window, I felt my heart drop as well. The first of Kiser's clan had left. Was Paul right about Kiser not caring about his whereabouts? I wasn't sure about that. Paul leaving because Mr. Kiser told him to would have been a different story, but Paul taking matters in his own hand and leaving on his own was soon going to stir up trouble. Sylvia just didn't think Mr. Kiser was going to let this rest. Before getting out of bed Sylvia prayed a long prayer. She asked the Lord to watch over Paul and she asked God to protect and guide him along the way. She also asked the Lord to shield Paul from seen and unseen danger. She knew that they all had suffered enough.

After getting dressed, she went to Sarah's room. She knew that she had to tend to her before she went to the still. Sarah moaned as Sylvia sat next to her in the dark room. Sylvia knew that she had sensed the difference and was probably wondering what she was doing there and not Paul. Paul couldn't find it in his heart to tell Sarah that he was leaving. He left this confession to be made by Sylvia. Sylvia had decided before going in there that she wasn't going to tell Sarah right away of Paul's departure.

Sarah appeared nervous and upset. She began spinning around and making loud noises. As Sylvia got closer, Sarah began banging her head on the walls as if she could escape through it. Sylvia grabbed her, but Sarah pushed her down at first. Sylvia stayed on the floor until she planned her next move. This time as she went toward Sarah, she tackled her and held her tight. Sarah tried to squirm out of the hold. As Sarah tried to bite Sylvia, Sylvia put her in a slight head lock and began to sing 'Yes Jesus Loves me' in her left ear. While in this position, Sylvia twisted her legs around Sarah's body and applied pressure. Sylvia didn't want to hurt her sister. She knew that Sarah only attacked her because she wasn't Paul. Since Sylvia could remember, Paul was the first to enter Sarah's room in the morning. Sylvia, Joseph and Mary would check on her from time to time, but Paul was the only consistent person in Sarah's life. Sarah began to calm down and after a lot of singing and rocking, Sarah was finally harmless and comfortable.

Sylvia bathed Sarah and brushed the kinks out of her hair. Sarah hadn't shed a tear yet. She ate her breakfast and looked out of the window even though there was no sun yet. Sylvia explained to her that she was going to go and empty her bucket and that she would be right back. Sarah just watched her every movement. Sylvia thought to herself, "If I could just get her to look into my eyes I think that she would trust me."

Sarah was squirming like a snake on the floor when Sylvia opened her door. "What are you doing?"

Sylvia had never seen or heard Sarah act like this. She was making a different sound than usual. It was a terrifying screeching noise. Something was definitely irritating her, but how was Sylvia to find out? Sarah pulled on her breeches and bit at her legs. "What's wrong with you?" asked Sylvia.

Sylvia was afraid and now she had wished that Paul had never left. She couldn't believe that only hours after Paul had left, something was wrong with her sister and she didn't know how to help her. She noticed that Sarah kept pulling at the backside of her breeches for the most part. Sylvia got down on the floor with Sarah and whispered, "Let me help you."

When Sylvia pulled down Sarah's breeches she fainted. When she awoke or came to the sun was out. With the sun being out she almost fainted again. What was coming out of Sarah's butt was now slithering across the floor. Sylvia counted three long ugly worms about twelve inches each. Sylvia looked at Sarah and all she saw was an alien. "What in the hell is going on? God if you get me out of this one, I owe you big time!"

Sylvia didn't want to alarm anyone of Paul's departure just yet so she ran over to Mr. Tyson and told him what was going on. She was relieved that Mr. Tyson wasn't worried. He told her that her sister had the worms. Mr. Tyson went into his shed and came back out with a mason jar of black liquid. Mr. Tyson said, "Give ya sister a mouth full of this twice a day. She'll pass all of those worms and feel a whole lot better."

Sylvia looked at the jar, opened it and smelled it and almost puked. "What is this, poison? Do you want me to kill Sarah?"

"I can't tell you all of my secrets, but it has some roots, aloe, and castor oil in it. I'm not telling you the rest, just like you won't tell anybody what you put in Kiser's shine."

Sylvia thanked Mr. Tyson and ran home to figure out how she was going to get Sarah to drink this stuff. Sarah was now lying on her bed asleep with her hand in her pants. The worms were dead on the floor. Sylvia didn't know what to make of this. As she was about to sit by Sarah, Joseph walked in and startled her.

"Where's Paul?" Joseph asked.

"I don't know. You haven't seen him yet this morning?"

"Nope. I came in here because Sarah was making too much noise. I knew that something was wrong. When I got in here she was passing worms again."

"She's done this before? I came in here and almost had a heart attack. I did faint and was surprise that no one heard me in here. I didn't know that this happened before. How come no one ever told me?"

"You live at the still, remember. Paul usually takes care of it. I don't know what he does, but he makes her feel better."

"I got something for the worms from Mr. Tyson. I just need your help to try and make Sarah drink this stuff. It's black and smells horrible."

"You told Mr. Tyson about Sarah? Are you crazy? Dad will kill you if he finds out!" yelled Joseph.

"Let's worry about Kiser later and help our sister." said Sylvia.

Joseph held Sarah while Sylvia squeezed both of Sarah's cheeks and poured in the mixture. It didn't go down easy, but they did their best to make sure that Sarah swallowed enough.

"I'm going to go and look for Paul. I don't like the fact that I haven't seen him and I don't trust dad. You be careful also because I heard that they busted an operation a few days ago. They said that there was a lot of police, bullets and buckshots. No one got killed, but several got hurt. They destroyed the still and took all of the shine. I hate that you are back there all alone and so far from the house. Even though we know that dad has connections with the police and pays them to cover his operation, I still don't like it. If anyone gets hurt, it will be you."

"Joseph, don't worry about me. I get up in that tree where I sit high and look low and ask God to protect me. He knows that being out there is not by my doing alone. I feel as though he placed me in these situations so he will be the one to bring me out. Don't you ever mention this to nobody, but I've wished many of times to get caught bootlegging for Kiser. I've often wondered if it would be my only way to get out of this here hell hole. I've prayed for John's safe return, I've done all that I can do. So whatever happens, I just say let his will be done."

"Okay Sylvia, but be careful." said Joseph. Then he hugged her.

Sylvia felt like she was going to faint for the second time that day. First Paul and now Joseph; did it take for them to feel the hate of Mr. Kiser to realize that she was worthy of love too?

Chapter 14

Sylvia was tired. She had stashed away several hundred gallons of moonshine that day. A local bootlegger was supposed to pick up this batch because there was a baseball game in the city that night. Mr. Kiser got really big orders when different events, especially sporting events were happening in the city. This was a good time for the people that never ventured out in the country to get their liquor. Sylvia made sure that she made the best stuff on the market, always sixty percent alcohol and clear to the last drop. She didn't know how she had perfected this skill so well. She had seen other people's products when they brought it by for Kiser to inspect. They wanted Kiser to tell them what they were doing wrong because their shine was so cloudy and when it wasn't cloudy, it had small particles floating around in there.

Mr. Kiser wasn't going to tell them if he knew, but the truth was, he didn't know. Mr. Kiser didn't have good shine until Sylvia began experimenting with his shine. Sylvia didn't believe in that Red Devil Lye, she preferred her shine to ferment slowly on its own. She also advised Mr. Kiser to invest in a good copper still, everyone was using old automobile radiators or an old used copper still that belonged to someone else. You know, one man's junk is another man's treasure.

89

Sylvia had just counted the cases of quart jars that Kiser sold at retail price when Joseph ran up. "Sylvia, something is terribly wrong. I still haven't found Paul and I don't believe that he has checked on Sarah yet because she is unusually loud today." Joseph said out of breath.

"Joseph, why are you so worried about Paul? He's a grown man now, I think that you have forgotten that."

"He's my brother! Do you know something that you are not telling me? It doesn't seem as though you're the least bit concern."

"I just think that he has run off with some little girl for the day. He was talking about someone he met at the country store a while ago. That's what I think."

"Come on, Paul of all people, with a girl."

"What's wrong with that? Who would have ever thought that we would have found you with a." Sylvia was so glad that she caught herself, but she knew that it was too late, because Joseph had already turned to leave. Her and her big mouth and she knew that she'd just opened up a fresh wound and poured salt in it.

"Joseph, I'm sorry come back!" yelled Sylvia.

As she sat with her back between two branches on the old gum tree she wondered how far Paul had gotten and if he was safe. She had wished that they hadn't spoken that day and that he didn't confess his love to her. She was way more worried than Joseph could imagine. Sylvia still didn't know how Mr. Kiser was going to react when he realized that Paul was nowhere to be found. She looked as far as she could see for any movement that could have been Paul. In her mind, she knew that her brother was long gone.

The grapes were getting sour and the apples were getting old. Why had she started adding all of these different fruits to her shine to add a little flavor. Mr. Kiser's customers loved it but it meant more work for her. Sylvia would make brandy when certain high price customers requested a shipment. It didn't matter what fruit she used, they loved it the same. While she was in the woods today she had also planned on picking some Life Everlasting. This was a herb that people added to their shine with lemon for a bad cold or a high fever. Whatever you had, this concoction would sweat it out of you overnight.

Sylvia needed it today because she had learned that when she smoked it, it took all of her worries away. She smoked it when she gave away Peter. She smoked it when John left. Sylvia smoked it after Kiser raped her. She smoked it the next day after any sexual intercourse with Kiser. After a day like today, she knew she was going to need to smoke it. If she could get away with it, she would smoke it around Sarah and maybe she would inhale just enough of it to calm her down. Sylvia knew that someone would pick up on the smell, but after hearing Joseph talk of how irritated Sarah is today, Sylvia knew that she couldn't go back to that house without some type of remedy. As bad as it sounded, Sylvia was going to try and get her sister high. Maybe this was just what the doctor ordered. If Joseph wanted a hit to calm his nerve she was going to make sure that she had enough for him too. There had to be away to escape the pain of being under a roof with Mr. Kiser besides running away. Paul had done this, but they all could do it. His moneymaker better not dare, at least not at the moment.

After talking with Paul and learning how he had ripped Kiser off and gotten away with it. Sylvia had also decided that she was going to start stashing away at least ten dollars a week. She was so stupid. Kiser didn't know how much shine she made or what he had orders for. Sylvia practically ran the operation from afar. He just made sure that she had enough corn, sugar, jars, jugs and whatever else she asked for to keep their operation running smoothly. When a driver slipped up on a delivery or didn't show up on time consistently, all Sylvia had to do was tell Mr. Kiser and that driver was through. So he respected her when it came down to business, because she was smart and careful. Sylvia believed that she was most clever when she smoked that herb she found to be so plentiful in the woods. She didn't need to go to that big city everyone talked about. When she was high, she sat in that tree and went all over the world and back.

When Sylvia reached the backyard, she sensed that there was trouble. Three or four men had just ran to the barn. Mr. Kiser had his shotgun across his shoulder looking at his corn field. Mr. Kiser shouted, "Paul, Paul, where is that damn boy?"

Sylvia didn't know what to do, but before she could turn around to go back into the woods, one of the men spotted her and said, "Hey, Kiser, there is your girl!"

"Sylvia, come here!" yelled Kiser. He was kicking rocks until she reached him. "Have you seen Paul at all today?"

"Paul, what's wrong with Paul?" questioned Sylvia.

"No one has seen him since last night. Did you see him before you left the house this morning?" asked Kiser.

"I heard him talking to Sarah earlier this morning before I left out."

"Are you sure, because Joseph told me that you fed Sarah this morning and not Paul?" asked Kiser.

"Joseph wasn't up yet when I heard Paul talking to Sarah. I'm sure that he will return sometime this evening and won't stay out all night."

"Look girl, don't play with me! Joseph said that you told him that Paul met some girl and he's possibly spending some time with her. You better tell me who she is and where I can find them!" shouted Kiser.

Sylvia had heard in Sunday school when she was younger that if you told one lie, then you had to keep telling lies to cover each lie. Now she was trying to think of what lie to tell now. "Well, you know Paul, he just told me about the girl he met, nothing more. So I wouldn't know which girl from Adam. Let's just hope that Paul is with her and that nothing has happened to him. Did you tell him any particular chores to do last night before you went to bed?"

"No, I didn't say much to anyone last night." Kiser said.

All of the other men listened from afar. Joseph came running and yelling words that we couldn't understand. This poor boy stuttered so badly, he couldn't get a girl to save his life, but I would have never thought he would stoop as low as getting busy with a dog. Joseph needed to calm down cause he was really frustrating Mr. Kiser. One of the men started laughing. It shocked them all when Kiser walked up to him and slapped him to the ground.

"No one laughs at a Kiser man, what's your problem? Do you want me to put these size fourteen in your behind or do you want me to cut your throat? Get your ass up and get the hell out of here! Now Joseph get over here and slow down! I don't want to hear that 'uuh-uuh' mess, you hear me?" Kiser said angrily.

"Pa-Pa-Pa-Paul, mu-mu-must have r-r-r-r-r-ran away! S-S-S-S-Some of his th-th-th-things are m-m-m-m-m-mis-s-s-s-sing!" stuttered Joseph.

"Runaway! Why the hell would Paul runaway? Show me what you're talking about!" said Kiser.

We all followed Joseph into the house. He went straight to the room which we shared. Everything looked in place to me; I didn't notice anything different about our room.

"See, his pillowcase is gone along with his blanket. I don't see his old Bible anywhere either. I believe a few pieces of his clothes are missing too. He doesn't have much clothes, but he has more than what's in that drawer down there." stuttered Joseph.

"I think you're right Joe! It looks like that son-of-a-bitch done ran away! If I find that bastard, I will kill him!"

"Wait Kiser!" screamed Mary. "What is all the commotion about? Are you looking for Paul or something?"

"Yes, I'm looking for Paul. That sucker done runaway! I'm going to bust his head to the white meat when I find him."

"Runaway! That's nonsense! Kiser men don't runaway! I couldn't find you this morning when I got the message. I found out that my sister Ester is very ill and they called for me. I knew that it was best for me to stay here and take care of the house and Sarah, so I told Paul to go for me. I gave him a few dollars and told him to hitch-hike rides until he got there. They said that she is pretty low and doesn't have anyone to look after her. You knew that she was the one to raise me when my mother could care less if I floated or sunk. I told him to stay only a few days and to return back because we need him around here. I was going to tell you once you came in from the fields, but I was in there fighting with Sarah all day and we both fell asleep after the fight was over. She is a strong girl!" explained Mary.

"And you are just telling me this! You should have ran out there and found me! How can you send him to the city and not ask me first?" Kiser slaps Mary. "Need him, who needs Paul around here? He can get the hell on if he wants to! Y'all heifers are crazy around here. I have to stay around this house more and get y'all back in check. I know y'all kids are half grown now, but lately y'all have forgotten who is king, including you Mary! If I have to start kicking y'all tails around here, I will. Mary, tell your little sissy that he can stay with Ester if he want to. Just tell him not to come back here pregnant!" Kiser roared.

Sylvia couldn't believe her ears. Now that Kiser believed that Paul didn't run away, he couldn't care less that Paul was gone just as Paul had said. What Sylvia couldn't believe even more was the fact that Mary lied to protect Paul. Had she known all along that Paul was gone? As Kiser left them all alone, Mary hugged Sylvia and whispered, "Sorry" in her ear.

95

Part 2

Chapter 15

Sylvia

For two weeks after Paul had left, we were practically beaten black and blue when we went in Sarah's room to tend to her. One day Mr. Kiser came in the house and heard all the rumbling and tumbling going on and he burst into Sarah's room like he was trying to rob somebody. He looked at us as if he was crazy when he saw me and momma in two separate corners planning our next move. Kiser called us, "Weak" and said that it was a shame for us to let one sick girl handle us in such a way. We just stared at him as he looked over at Sarah. Sarah was a mess. She hadn't bathed in a week and smelled of funk. She didn't want us to touch her or come near her. All Sarah wanted was Paul. She couldn't say it with her words, but it was in her voice and the look was in her eyes.

As we would open her door very slowly to enter her room, Sarah would wait quietly, watching and waiting for Paul to come in. Once she realized that the person entering her room wasn't Paul, she would start all that hem and a hawing. Screaming screams that one had never heard. She was dangerous for all involved, including herself. She bucked like a donkey and climbed like a monkey. She had unbelievable strength. Sarah had stopped using the

99

bathroom in her bucket and now peed and pooped wherever she pleased. The entire house smelled foul, and Mr. Kiser wanted us to do something about that awful stink smell that lingered throughout the house all day long. We had explained to Kiser Sarah's recent aggressive behaviors, but he just lashed out at us even more and said, "I don't care what she does to you, but y'all better get this smell out of my house! If you think that she is going to kick y'all behind, then you better think about the beating y'all will get from me if y'all don't clean that mess up in there! Mary, if you can't handle Sarah, then you better get that faggot back here tomorrow, cause this never happened before Paul went to your old, ugly sister!"

So here it was days later and he had walked in on momma and me trying our best to do what we were told to do. Mr. Kiser looked at the three of us with disgust. This was probably his first time in Sarah's room in fifteen years. He had to be shocked looking into the eyes of a female version of him. Sarah had grown to look just like her daddy. Looked like him so much that she was ugly.

"How in the hell did y'all let this retard ruin my house like this? The hog pen out back doesn't look or smell like this and I have over twelve dozen hogs out there. Somebody done lost their freakin mind! I knew she was dumb all along, but I see for myself that she is a total retard! She has to go! Mary, she is out of here, today. You hear me Mary! This is what you get for sending that sissy off to help your sister! Now your animal will have to pay the price for your stupid decision!"

Mr. Kiser came in the room and went directly for Sarah. He didn't ask us anything! I had a gut feeling that he was going to really hurt my sister and I wasn't sure if this is what I really wanted to happen. No one had bruised me up like Sarah did, but I still didn't want Kiser to hurt her. She didn't understand what was going on, at least that's what we've always assumed. I wished for Paul at this very moment and wished that he had never left us. I said a silent prayer. Who would have known that my prayer would change the events that I expected to occur in Sarah's room that day.

As soon as Kiser grabbed Sarah, Sarah tossed him, lifted his head up and placed him in a head lock. When I saw his tongue hanging out and the seat of his pants were wet, that's when I jumped up, "Sarah No!"

I ran toward them and Sarah must have seen the fear in my eyes because she let Kiser go and ran into the opposite corner of her room. She sat with her knees to her chest, rocking back and forth humming, "Yes, Jesus loves me."

Momma and I tried our best to get Kiser out of there while Sarah wasn't paying us any attention. This took some time because we both were afraid that Sarah would jump on us and was convinced that she was strong enough to beat our brains out. We dragged him out like he dragged the pigs out of the pen after he had slaughtered them. Kiser's body had no fight left. We were afraid, Lord please don't let Kiser be dead down here on this floor. Could the only man that I had known as my father be dead! We dragged him until we got Kiser to his bedroom. Momma said to keep pulling him because if we have to call for help, it would be better if Kiser was in his room. The people of Deer Island had forgotten about Sarah. The only person that had seen her in fifteen years besides the people that lived in the house with her was the nurse. Mr. Kiser had threatened the nurse years ago that she better not tell a soul that Sarah was still around or of her conditions. What a shame that would be on the Kiser's name. Especially since the Kisers always was in competition with the Joneses since they all could remember.

We don't know how we did it, but we picked Kiser's dead weight off of the floor and placed him in his bed. The comfort of his bed enabled Kiser to get out a yakking cough, or maybe he was playing dead out of fear of Sarah attacking his butt again. Those slimy coughs sounded like music to our ears. Kiser dead would have been fine by me, but Sarah being the cause of his death would have put me under his grave. I would have somehow felt responsible for his death; because I promised Paul that I would take care of Sarah. To have Sarah punished for the death of her father would have been cruel and unexplainable, especially when the world didn't know Sarah was still a part of it, at least not on Deer Island.

Momma nursed Kiser back to conscious by wiping his face and head with a very damp cloth. She even breathed into his mouth a bit to jump start whatever it was that needed to be jump started. We sat him up propped on two pillows. Then momma told him what had just happened. For the first time in my life, I witness Mr. Kiser not being able to say a mumbling word. I even saw tears in his eyes, but I wasn't sure if that was tears from the choking that Sarah had put on him or tears from his emotion built up inside. When he finally spoke, he asked, "Why didn't anyone tell me?"

"We tried to tell you!" we both said in unison.

"When?" Kiser asked.

"When you told us that we better do something about Sarah's room and that awful smell that you could smell all through the house!" said Momma.

"I'm not talking about all that fighting and screaming y'all told me about!" Kiser said.

"Well, tell you about what?" asked momma.

"That she looked just like me! At first I thought that I was seeing myself in the mirror, until I blinked."

"I don't know Kiser. I guess we didn't think that you would care or agree. She been look like you all the time. It's just that when you saw her last at the age of five or six, she was still a baby." Momma explained.

"Why is she so evil? How did she get so strong?" questioned Kiser.

"Only God knows the answer to those questions," mom answered.

"We can't keep her here Mary, she'll hurt somebody," Kiser said.

The very next morning I ran out of the house before the mice had finished collecting the crumbs from the night before. I had thought about this too many times not to give it a try. I went to my stash and got to rolling. I had learned that there was a science to the rolling just like I had learned as a young child that there was a science to making good liquor. I smoked a little before going back to the house because I needed to ease my mind and prepare me for my flight or fight; whichever was waiting for me. I don't know how Paul did this for so long, but I respected him a whole lot more now than I ever did before.

I was also happy that Mr. Tyson had walked over a few days ago with a letter for me. It was from Paul. Paul wrote that he wasn't where he wanted to settle down and that he would continue to venture on as the time permitted him to. He was gone now for two weeks and was certain that he was at least two hundred miles away which was still too close to Deer Island for him. Paul said that he hadn't ran into much hard times and that the money he had was coming in handy to get him where he needed to go. He said that he had told several people about my shine and that it was the best in the world. Paul wrote that all the people seemed very anxious to try some of my brew. He warned me not to be surprised if I got in a few big orders in the near future from unknown customers. Paul advised that this would be a great time for me to start getting my money off of the top and stashing it away and then blessing Kiser with the rest. With moonshine being illegal, we didn't care too much about new customers. New customers sometimes meant trouble, being that this was the best way the police knew how to set moonshiners up.

Paul hoped that Sarah was coming along and that I had remembered to sing to her like he told me to do. Paul also expressed his concerns about Mr. Kiser and what he must have said and done once he realized that he was gone. In his letter, Paul explained why he mailed the letter to Mr. Tyson's address. He told me to make sure and destroy the letter and the envelope as soon as I was through reading it. He knew that Kiser was the only person allowed to touch his mailbox and if he saw a letter addressed to anyone else that came in, he would be the first to read it, and probably the only one to read it. Oh how he made his own family feel like slaves.

"Lousy Bastard!!" I yelled. I destroyed the envelope which was stamped, South Carolina. So, Paul still had a ways to go, but I kept the letter. I had to keep Paul's letter. Just looking at his handwriting gave me the hope I needed to survive.

Chapter 16

If I had known this plant was going to make my life this easy, I would have made a nest out of life everlasting and slept in it. I could not believe that something so wild, plentiful and free was the answer to our prayers since the day Paul left. I didn't tell anybody, I kept it to myself, and now Momma, Joseph and Mr. Kiser were worshiping the ground that I walked on.

I was so glad that I thought about my approach first before ever going back to the house. I didn't know how I was going to get Sarah to ever smoke life everlasting when she had never smoked anything in her life. Kiser had her penned up in her room so long, I wondered if she'd ever seen someone smoke a cigarette or pipe before in her life.

Taking a few puffs of it is what got me to thinking of my plan while I was still out there in the woods. I found that this herb had that affect on me when I smoked it. It did nothing of the sort when I would drink it for a terrible cold. When I smoked it, it cleared my head and all of my worries ran free. My feet didn't ache, I didn't worry about Pete and John, and I laughed even when I knew there was nothing in my life worth smiling about. Life Everlasting had become known to be my "Grace and Mercy," because nothing that Pastor Baker preached about meant anything to me since Paul revealed to me that holy bastard was my real father. I wanted so badly to turn Sarah loose on him the next time he stopped by our house. The last time he dropped by, he walked in and asked my mother, "Are you ready to put this bread in the oven." I watched her smile and grab the seat of Pastor Baker's pants. I threw up right there, peeking around the corner.

I had to admit, when I think back to the scene where Sarah had tossed Kiser and was choking his fat, thick, almost white tongue out of his head, I do feel a little thrill run up my spine. If it was someone else's hands and not Sarah's, I probably would have wished for his death. The Kiser that I had known was always such a cruel man. I don't believe he has ever loved a soul.

When I got near Sarah's door, I stopped and listened to determine what she was probably doing in there at that very moment. It seemed like she knew that I was there and was waiting for me to open her door. As I knelt down to her door, I felt her presence on the other side. I pulled the rolled herb out and lit it, placing it at the bottom of Sarah's door. I took a few puffs which allowed it to burn better producing more fumes. I allowed most of the fumes to flow under Sarah's door. When she saw the smoke, I could see her in front of her door. I tried my best not to inhale anymore of the fumes, knowing that I still needed a level head once I decided to enter Sarah's room. I let the entire roll burn until it had diminished.

I sat quietly for ten minutes right outside Sarah's door before entering her room. I knocked at first, but got no response. I eased my way in. Sarah was sitting on the floor twirling her hair, which looked like matted wool. She looked up at me, but didn't move or scream. Sarah appeared calm for the first time in her life. I sat down beside her and lit another smoke. I didn't call it a joint or reefer because it wasn't marijuana and because of Mr. Tyson we all knew what marijuana was.

I pretended to smoke it hoping that Sarah was watching me out of the corners of her eyes. When I knew she was indeed watching me, I puffed on it for real causing the smoke to travel a zigzag formation up to the ceiling. Sarah startled me very badly when she reached over and snatched my smoke right out of my mouth. She placed it in hers and drew on it until her eyes sunk back deep in her head. When Sarah let it go, she moaned and dropped it to the floor while falling over on her stomach.

Sarah lied there giggling so hard that I had to laugh, but while I laughed I was also crying. I cried from way deep down in the pits of my belly. I was crying because I don't believe just like I for the first time, Sarah had never heard herself laugh, laugh until her soul was washed white as snow.

Sarah was in a daze for several hours. I used this time to first clean up her room, because I realized that it wasn't going to do anybody any good to clean up Sarah if I had to leave her in this filth. After cleaning the room, I gave her a good washing with a tub of hot water and what I called "man soap." It was a soap that only Mr. Kiser used that hung from a rope. I used this soap because every time Kiser took a bath with it the entire house smelt like it and Sarah needed something strong besides just the bleach I had added to her bath water. After a good bath and her hair comb, Sarah fell asleep.

While Sarah was sleeping, I ran into the kitchen and made her a huge lunch because I knew from experience that she was going to be extremely hungry after that smoke wore off of her; which was pretty soon. I placed her food before her without disturbing her sleep. I didn't want to be in there once she woke up and was no longer high from my Grace and Mercy.

I went back in to check on her after I came back in from doing my chores. Hours had passed so I didn't know what to expect. I eased the door open and I slipped in since I didn't hear any commotion. Sarah watched my every move, but she didn't move an inch. I went over to her and sat beside Sarah. Sarah dropped her head and looked to the floor. I began to sing very softly, "Yes Jesus loves me." Sarah began humming the tune along as I sung. I couldn't believe my ears. We were finally communicating, even if it was through song. I found that much better than listening to the robins that I had heard sing time and time again.

When I stopped singing, Sarah didn't look at me, but I couldn't believe my ears when she said, "More!" I sung until I sung my big sister sound asleep. When she woke up the next morning ranting and raving, I had her smoke ready. That was all it took to calm her right on down.

Everyone had asked me what was that smell. I told them all that it was something I was using to keep the smell down in Sarah's room. Mr. Kiser and momma thought the smell was familiar but neither one of them could identify the smell so I just let by gone be by gone. Sooner or later they would find out that it was just what the DR. had ordered to heal my sweet sister Sarah. So that is what I called it every morning when I brought it to her. "Sarah, it is time for your medicine."

Chapter 17

One Year Later

What was I to do? Mr. Jones had driven by early this morning before the sun had come up and yelled from his truck hoping that I would hear him. "Sylvia, Sylvia, if you can hear me, look out the window!" Mr. Jones and Mr. Kiser hated the grounds that each other walked on. They were parted in fight once and promised if the other crossed the other's path, someone would definitely be killed. Sylvia knew this was the root of why Kiser made her give up Peter more than any other reason that he could name. Having a child for Mr. Jones' son was the wickedest of the wickedest in the eyes of Kiser.

Mr. Jones somehow learned at an early age that it was better to work smarter than work harder. He had a huge farm of his own and he barely had to lift a finger. He hired quality farmhands that made sure that they earned a profit. He wasn't cheap like Mr. Kiser, only the least fit would work for Kiser's wages.

I heard the yelling and tried to get to my window before Mr. Kiser silenced it all with his shotgun. First I tried to look out of my window to identify the yeller. The glass was too foggy to see out of so I took my chances and quickly upped the window before the truck sped off. My mouth fell open when I recognized the driver. It was Mr. Jones. Once he saw me, he yelled out again. "I'm on my way to the train station to pick up John! I thought that I would let you know. He said that he wrote you several letters in the past year and there was no response. So he figured you never got any of them, and he stopped writing you."

I couldn't respond because I couldn't believe my ears. Was John coming home? Was John coming back here to Deer Island? Was John coming back here today? Unbelievable! Before pulling off, Mr. Jones yelled for the last time, "He is coming back for you!" Then he drove off and left me just in a blank stare. Why couldn't I say anything? Mr. Jones probably thinks that I'm such a jerk. I have been dreaming of this day for years and when I hear that my dreams are coming true, I can't say a mumbling word. Wow!

I continued looking out the window, staring at the very spot where we'd last hugged and kissed. I couldn't believe it. Years had gone by and now those feelings were coming back as if it had been yesterday. Where had time gone? I was now eighteen years old and hadn't seen the inside of a school since I had Peter. Did I spend all those years up in a tree in the woods making shine?

As I was about to close my window, I heard the strangest cry that could come from any animal. What in the hell was going on this time of morning. It was practically still dark out here. The sound was getting closer and louder as I tried my best to look through the fog. I saw headlights approaching, but that didn't explain the noise that I heard. It was Kiser's truck for sure. No wonder he didn't hear Mr. Jones earlier. He was up and gone already. What was he doing out so early? I used to listen for his every move once he started having sex with me a couple of years ago, always hoping that he wasn't coming to get me. After his encounters with the hag rides at night, Kiser stopped sleeping with me after he realized that the hag only rode him every time he forced himself on top of me. After he didn't touch me for awhile, I was able to sleep without worry, and I thanked God for sending the hag.

I couldn't believe my eyes. Mr. Kiser had hooked a chain to his bumper and was pulling a dog down the paved road. The dog was howling for dear life as his fur and flesh was being left behind him. I swear I only saw two legs left on the dog as Kiser passed by, not even noticing me hanging out my window. I guess he had found out whom or what was responsible for slaughtering his chickens the past few nights. Mr. Kiser was upset all week because his chickens were being slaughtered at night. Some animal was digging under the fence and getting into his chicken coop and this made him really mad. It was one thing to get in there and kill one or two chickens for a meal, but something was getting in there and slaughtering ten to fifteen at a time and just leaving them there. I guess Kiser wanted the dog to suffer before he died. Sylvia had seen Kiser kill many animals for disturbing his farm, but it was always a shot to the head. He was really mad this time. I hope this was the dog that was responsible for killing at least forty of Kiser's hens. If not, he'd come around like a thief in the night for the last time.

Sylvia now felt like God was putting everything in its proper order, because the entire time Mr. Jones was yelling outside in the front of Kiser's house her heart was swelling full of blood because of her fear of Mr. Kiser hearing him. She knew this was the reason why words could not escape from her mouth. All of her fear was fading away as she thought about Mr. Jones' last words, "He's coming back for you!" The nerve of Mr. Kiser to not give me my letters. She now wondered if Paul had sent her any more letters. She knew that Mr. Tyson had brought her three, which he mailed to Tyson's address because Paul knew his daddy. In his last letter, he stated that he was safe and still trying to establish himself. He said that he would not send for me and Sarah until he was settled. He kept trying to convince me that the streets were no place for the ladies. I worried about Paul, cause I knew that under his skin, he wasn't tougher than me or Sarah.

Enough with all of this. My Johnny was coming home and he was coming to get me. My mind, heart, and soul now craved the only man that I ever had feelings for. I loved him with a double portion of love, because I longed all my life to be loved and he was the only someone to love me. I only wished that he could come back for me and Peter, but I knew for myself that my child was getting the best of care and an abundance of love. What else could a poor, abused, uneducated, bastard of a mother ask for? It didn't matter, I still loved my baby!

I soaked in the tub scrubbing my hair, heels, and everything in between. I didn't know what John expected from me. He had probably changed a great deal. He had seen the world and everything in it. Mr. Tyson tried to convince me on several occasions that John would find a beautiful, worldly woman out there and make her his wife. I cried myself to sleep many nights and began to accept this, preparing myself for the worst. I would rather John come back to Deer Island in a body bag than to come back here in love with some other woman. So I began to pray and ask God to save my John for me. Again, I have to say, "Thank you Jesus!" I'm so glad that I didn't let what I had found out about Pastor Baker turn me against the Lord, because I found refuge in my Father, the Devine and Holy Spirit.

I wished that I had something nice to put on. It's funny how this is the first time I had ever felt this way. I hadn't cared about my appearance until now. All along I had killed this person inside of me. She didn't exist, not until Mr. Jones stopped by this morning and woke her up. As I laid back in the tub, I began to sing, "Yes, Jesus Loves Me." I was really feeling this song until I realized that I was now sitting in a tub of cold water. Just as I was about to get out, I heard Kiser yell at the bathroom door, "Come out of there, before I kick this damn door down!" This was the ticket that I needed to say, "Kiser go straight to hell!" Paul was gone. What was he going to do once he learned that I would soon be gone too? That's when I thought of Sarah.

"I'm coming out now, one more second please! I had a hag on my back last night and I'm still trying to get that feeling off of me." I told this to Kiser hoping that it would buy me some more time. I had learned him well throughout the years and had found out that he really wasn't crap! He acted mean and tough, but if a rat ran near him, he would probably jump up on a chair, and of course the rat had to die later.

"Sylvia, hurry up. I have to take care of some business today! If you cause me to be late, I'm going to be that hag that rides you next. Did you see that big order that we need for the baseball game in Charleston on Friday night? They said that they want my premium stuff. So you better hook it up!" Mr. Kiser was saying all of this from behind the bathroom door.

Truth is I was afraid to come out because of the way I smelled and how clean I looked. Now that I knew Kiser was going to be busy, I really didn't want him finding out about John's arrival and spoiling everything for me. Now I wonder what he was going to be busy doing. A typical day for Kiser is keeping up his farm, but today he talked like he was going to be doing a whole lot more, and it didn't sound like he was going to be here.

I opened the door and Kiser said, "What's that smell? What were you doing in here? Why were you in the tub, and not taking your usual bird bath in the sink? How did you get your skin so clean?"

The truth be told, the last couple of years I wanted to appear a little dirty to keep Kiser off of me. I can remember when I use to leave residue on me when I wiped so that I could smell awful when Kiser tried to lay on me. I made myself undesirable just to keep him away from me. Along with the hag thing, it seemed to work. Hell, I was tired of being stink and dirty just to keep a stink and dirty man away from John's goods. I really hoped that's what he expected me to be. I rushed passed Kiser because I didn't have time for his mess today. It wasn't until I got in my room and read the note from my mom that she had snuck in there while I was in the bathroom that I remembered that today was my birthday. She had written me a note which said, "Happy Birthday to my favorite child. I love you!" I couldn't believe it, John must have planned this day. I was nineteen today, and this was going to be my best birthday ever.

I bet John had really planned this day for his return, because I can remember like yesterday, John and I going to his mother's grave on my birthday when we were children because Doris, John's mother and I shared the same birthday. We always felt like God meant for us to be for all these little similarities like these. I spent several hours with him at his mother's grave listening to him talk to her. John was really a good guy. No matter what he was told, he loved his mom, always did, and always would. Doris Jones was John's queen and I was probably second after her.

Kiser appeared to be running when I saw him dash into the kitchen. I had never seen Kiser in such a rush. He said that he had to be somewhere and he definitely was trying to get there, but where? He didn't mention anything about the dog he had dragged to pieces hours ago. He was such a hateful man and I knew all too well how hateful he really was. I still saw the way he looked at me with his lustful eyes. I saw the desire in his eyes this morning and again I say, "Thank you Jesus for sending that Hag, which I do believe was Mr. Tyson's old soul." Sometimes it looked like Mr. Tyson would be talking to me about any little thing, but somehow it seemed like his eyes could see straight through me and I was afraid of what my soul was revealing to him.

As soon as Kiser left the house, Mr. Jones truck came riding by. He stopped right in front of our house. I assumed that he must have passed Kiser on the way in and knew that it was safe for him to just pull-up in our front yard. I couldn't help myself, I ran out of the door with my wings flapping in the air. I was flying and I only had one runway I was landing on, the one that had the key to my heart. As I got near the truck, the passenger door opened and there was John sitting there not moving. I stopped and realized that I now was scared. I'd never thought about John's condition after fighting years in the war. Was John alright? Was he missing a leg, arm, or an eye? I didn't know and I didn't care. I just wanted John back here in Deer Island, so that we could start off where we left off.

Now I was really worried. John still hadn't moved so I began walking slowly to the truck. Why was he doing this to me? I hope John wasn't having second thoughts about coming back home to me. I could now see him sitting there clear as day looking at me. Mr. Jones was looking at me too. Why were they staring at me? I was out of breath as I reached for John when I finally was standing right in front of the passenger door.

"My, my, my," was all that John could say. He looked like everything was still intact as I glimpsed over him quickly. We hugged and kissed for what seemed liked minutes. Then John broke the silence by asking me, "So, is this how you have been coming out of the house all of these years while I was gone?"

"What are you talking about John?" I asked.

"Look at you. I have never in my life seen a woman run out of the house before in her underwear and bra. You looked so comfortable doing it too. With that big butt and those plump full titties, girl you are so beautiful! Sylvia, will you marry me?" John fell to his knees with his hands on my behind.

"Oh, No!" I said.

"No!" yelled John. "And why can't you marry me?"

"No, I meant, oh no I don't have any clothes on! I didn't realize that I ran out of the house like this. Kiser left and I saw your dad's truck pull up and I lost my mind. I can't believe I have been standing out here like this! Now I see why y'all just stared at me when I was running over here. I thought something was wrong with you!"

"Lady shut up and answer me please!" said John.

"Answer you?" I asked.

"Will you marry me?" John asked again still on bended knee.

"Yes, yes, yes, but let me put on some clothes before this gets out all over Deer Island that Sylvia was so desperate, that she got naked for John at his arrival."

"Okay, go inside and get dressed and come right back out. I'm going to let daddy go on home, and I'll be out here waiting for my lady!"

"Welcome home Baby!" Sylvia ran into the house and her heart was pounding. From what she felt in her panty, she believed that her heart probably thought that it would drown in her wetness. Things were happening too fast, but she didn't want it to slow down one bit.

It seemed like God had took forever to start even thinking about answering her prayers, but now that He saw fit to bless her, she just wanted all her blessings to rain down on her. She knew that she could stand the rain. Her life had suffered from the drought for way too long. God had delivered John back to her and he figured that it was all in God's plans because he knew that Sylvia could not wait but for so long to know if John indeed was still hers for the taking. So, God couldn't plan it any other way than for John to propose right then and there. Did John actually think that Sylvia's answer could have been "No?" Seriously, Sylvia would have done cartwheels if she had some clothes on. Since she had ran her thick butt out of the house in her drawers and bra, she had to walk very stupidly back into the house. She now wondered what Mr. Jones thought of her. He probably felt as though she had lost her marbles, especially since he was aware of how Kiser was and what he was most likely capable of. Sylvia was ashamed, but damn happy!

Chapter 18

God had spoken of deliverance, redemption and being cared for. In His words he said that you have to watch, pray, and be ready when it comes. God said, "He will deliver, but you have to believe within your heart that He will deliver!" I knew that I had been purchased by the blood of Jesus Christ and the way for me had been paid for, cause He died for me and you. Kiser held me captive long enough. He would no longer be able to get in my way of happiness. I could see my pathway clearer. At this moment I felt like Jeremiah, fire shut up in my bones.

I was now dressed and ready to run out there and face the world. I walked out on the porch and looked around for John. I didn't see him anywhere. If he'd left, I was going to kill him. I sure couldn't find him, but I hadn't looked anywhere but as far as my eyes could see. So, I walked around the house and there he stood, looking eyes to eyes with Sarah as she stood at her window. Neither of them was saying a word, due to Kiser having her window chained and bolted up. She was a prisoner in her own room and I could tell by the look on John's face that she would be a prisoner no more once he had done whatever was in his heart to do about this situation. I waved at them both. John walked over to me and asked the question, "WHY? How could you all let this be?"

"John, you know that Kiser's ways are the law around here while he's alive and well! He hasn't changed. Only time has changed!" I answered.

"Did Kiser do anything to you to hurt you while I was gone?" John asked while looking deep into my eyes.

"No!" I said in a hurry.

"My, my, did you answer that fast! Don't make me kill that Joker my first day back!" John said very angrily.

We both looked back at Sarah and began walking away. John led me to the barn, a place that we both knew all too well. Nothing had changed much about the farm since John last saw it. Kiser didn't give a damn about physical features. John pushed me against the wall and began kissing me the way I had dreamed he would. John looked into my eyes and kissed my forehead. "I've missed you. There is no other like you in this world. I searched high and low and still couldn't find anybody. I looked to the east and I looked to the west and I still didn't find anybody better than you. It is you that complete me Sylvia. I love you!"

We both looked over to the ladder which led to the loft where we use to play. John grabbed my hand and led me there. We ran up the steps and I took pleasure in John ripping my clothes off. I felt my insides gushing out. The juices of my berry were flowing and it was sweeter than honey. John's manhood, now stood out like old Mr. Mule's in the stable below us. I had never noticed his parts before because I didn't have another to compare it to. I now thought about Kiser and his little short wiener and I almost pushed John away. This was not the time to let this horrible fool steal my joy. Why was John pushing two of his fingers inside of me? This was all too different. He licked my breast and sucked on my nipples. What was a poor farm girl to do? My body felt like my furnace as I brewed my own juices. This was more potent than any of my shine. Then John entered me, I held him in and started to tremble. I trembled and cried, because I could not find anybody greater, greater than He! I knew that this was sin, but I was still giving God all of the glory!

John broke my concentration when he said, "Sylvia, get on top of me!"

"What?"

"Get on top of me and ride me baby!" John said.

"John, I don't know what you're talking about!"

John laid down beside me with his manhood in his hand and said, "Come sit on me and let me show you. It will feel good, you'll see."

I climbed up on top of him and he grabbed my hips pushing me back and forth and up and down. After a few more pushes, I pushed him back and I rocked him like one of old Mister's rocking chair. Every once and a while, John yelled, "Sylvia!"

I wasn't going to question where John had gotten some of his ideas because I knew before he left Deer Island, he would just push himself inside me and move in and out, in and out. But on his first day back, he had asked me to, "Get on top, get on your knees, stand up, bend over, put your feet here, suck it, bite it, lick it, and swallow it!" My body was worn, but I liked it and loved him. I did wonder who had taught him all of those tricks and was he missing her?

Thank God that Kiser had left for today, because we had no disruptions or fear. As we left the barn, John began to say his goodbyes for the time being. He had stopped by to see his Love first, but there were others he needed to see. He spoke of how he had reflected on his childhood and how his life could have been so different if Doris had not been killed so tragically. John told me how his anger toward her unknown killer enabled him to gun down many men during the war those others left standing. He said that he was their best sniper, if he saw it move, he killed it. He shared with Sylvia that he had told not a soul during the war or his departure about his mother. John loved his mother, and Mr. Jones and Sylvia knew best.

John told Sylvia how he had planned his return today, because he wanted his two most favorite women in this world to be happy for their birthday. He said that he wanted to be the one that made them smile. John told Sylvia that he was through with the Army and that he was home for good. John was now heading to Doris's grave and he wanted to go alone. He explained to me that he needed this time for him and Doris alone. As he walked away, John looked back and said, "When I come back, I want us to go and see my boy!" Tears began to roll down my face. Then I began to pray that Peter would remember his real father. All of this had to be happening for a really good reason, and I now knew that it all was in God's plan.

Chapter 19

John

What the hell is that man doing here? I've never known anyone to visit my mother's grave but me and daddy. I left daddy home plowing his fields because he just felt overjoyed that his only child was home. My father had never married or had any more kids after my mother's death. He tells people that he got over losing my mother, but the truth is, we never got over her horrific death. It is just so hard to come to grips knowing that she died so unhappy. My mother was full of love, but never knew for herself what love really was. Love was having a baby boy that you brought into this world and nursed him by your breast to make him strong. She cuddled with me at night and sang me sweet lullabies while holding me against her heartbeat at night, praying that I would fall asleep and stay asleep for at least four hours. Love was teaching me how to potty and dress myself when I got up in the mornings. A mother's love taught me how to pray before bedtime, and kissed me before going to sleep.

I loved my mama and for over twenty years I've tried to keep these memories of her sacred in my heart, because I knew this was all that I had left since that dark morning I heard the officer tell my dad that my mama was dead. I heard my father crying many nights, because he knew that Doris died looking for a father which she believed would make her complete.

The man at my mother's grave was talking out loud as if he'd never expected anyone to come out there that day. Who the hell could this be at my mother's grave? He sounded wounded and was sobbing. After realizing this, I just stood back behind an old oak tree and listened. I had a lot to say to my mother on this day and I wanted to apologize to her for not coming by in years because of my departure. But she knew that I was away making sure that she would be proud of me. I could still remember her praying over me the night before she left us. She prayed to God asking him to protect her child whenever she wasn't near. This is the prayer that I have always kept close and dear to my heart. I knew that because of her prayer, I had survived the war and was going to survive the war.

Whoever this man was, he was hurting and torn. I heard it in his voice as he spoke so deeply to the grave. I could hear him pleading for forgiveness. I wanted to pull out my pistol and put a bullet in his head. Could this be my mother's killer? I am about to kill an American on American soil, but something within me told me to be quiet and listen some more to hear what he had to say. I heard him say, "I would give everything that I have away to have you back here again. Even though the world believes that I have everything, I feel as though I have nothing. I love you more than anything I have in my life right now. Doris, I'm so sorry. I watched from afar as you grew from a baby to a beautiful lady, but I couldn't come near you."

John listened as the man continued to talk to his mother's grave, "I remember as if it was yesterday, your mother and I couldn't hide what we had done from anyone no longer. Her stomach which was flatter than an old washboard was now protruding as if she'd swallowed a small honeydew melon. We were both kids ourselves in the eyes of some. Your mom was fifteen and I, sixteen. Back then we grew up fast, had to work to help out the family you know. At the young age of nine, my old man had me out the house before the sun came out trying to earn a penny to contribute to our house. Your mother loved that in me. I was a hard, humble worker and she knew that I was going to make a great husband one day. Doris, I loved your mother very much, and she loved me the same. When she realized that she was pregnant, she was scared. She told me that this baby was going to be a death sentence for her. So she begged me to run off with her, so that we could live happily ever after. I convinced her that our life was no fairy tale, and we both would starve together and our baby would die along with us. We both knew how hateful her father was. Before falling in love with your mother, she had shared with me many stories of being beaten and dragged by her mean father. Your grandfather was a hateful man. The only reason your mom and I spent time together was because we both worked on Mister's plantation in his cotton field. I would see her come dragging in many mornings as if she had struggled all night long. One day as a tear fell from her eye, I saw a twinkle that I will never forget. I reached over and kissed her that day for the first time. I kissed her for enduring the pain that I knew only she could. I saw the strength that she possessed. I fell in love with your mom and God as we prayed many nights together before departing for our separate homes. We knew that only God could bring us through what we had created."

"One morning your mom came to the field late, which was unusual for her. She pulled me to the side and told me that I had to help her get away soon before her father found out about the baby. She said that her dad was beating her and her mom just to have something to do at night. He was known to most as an alcoholic, mostly working only for a drink those days. The abuse of the alcohol made him insane and dangerous. I was terrified of his evil spirit, but I couldn't tell your mom how frightened I was of him. She needed to feel protected. So I continued to pray asking God to see us through, even though I knew that we too had sinned. So your mother continued to cover and hide her belly for as long as she could. We had decided that we loved each other and our unborn child too much to visit one of the witch doctors on the island that snatched out babies with hooks and hangers, which caused their death and sometimes left the women dead, paralyzed, or poisoned themselves."

John couldn't believe what he was hearing, so he just stood behind the old oak tree which hid him completely, quietly listening to what the man he now knew as Doris's father had to say. Tears filled his eyes and fire burned his heart. He had never felt this bad watching a soldier die during the war.

"On the night that your grandfather found out about your mom's pregnancy, he was drunk. He smelled of pee and corn liquor. Neither I nor your mom knew what we were in store for. Even though I tried all I could to show him the good in me, he hated me because I was a Kiser! I was a humble young guy, never did any harm to anybody. I had never hurt a fly, but all your father saw in me was a Kiser man. He told me to stay away from his daughter, because he said that I would ruin her. 'Once a Kiser, always a Kiser, you all are all the same!' is what he said."

"So that night, he fought me like a man. Your grandfather kicked and punched me in my balls. I felt my balls roll up into my guts as I fell to the floor. I tasted blood in my mouth, but couldn't remember him ever hitting me there. He then grabbed your pregnant mother, while you were still kicking strong inside her belly. He choked his only daughter as he stuck himself deep within her from behind, ravaging her as if he was trying to plunge you out of her. I got up off of the floor and ran toward them as I listened to the only person that ever loved me, cry out with all she had screaming and begging me to run away. Once in reach of her, your grandfather slammed me into the floor then pushed your mother down on the wooded kitchen table and raped her some more."

"I was so weak back then, nothing like the man I had become some thirty years ago. I was hurt and was spitting up blood. What happened next after watching your grandfather rape your mother changed my life forever! That drunk grabbed me, pushed me up against the splintered walls, looked me in my eyes and said, 'She is mine and I told you to stay away from her. See what happens when you spoil another man's goods? You damaged her, just knocked her up. You Kisers think that you can have everything your way. I'm sick and tired of your crap Kiser, and tonight I'm putting an end to it! You came around here and did this to my daughter, got her knocked up! I guess y'all thought that I was too wasted to notice her coming out of her skin. You didn't think that I would recognize that there was a baby growing in her gut. You took advantage of what belonged to me. Now I'm going to show you exactly how

I felt when I realized that you had messed with something that didn't belong to you even after I had told you to stay away from her. I warned you Kiser, but no, you had to knock her up like she belonged to you! Are you happy now, cause you are going to be a Pappy?' was what he asked me."

"I couldn't say a word. I had already peed in my pants and my heart was pounding against the wall of my chest. I looked at your mother as she bled right there in front of me. Your grandmother had run for help awhile ago and had not returned. I was so ashamed when that hateful bastard pulled down my pants that I didn't grasp what was about to happen to me. Right there in front of your mother who was losing more blood by the minute, that beast rammed his hardness into me. I threw up everything that was in me. For a period of time I believed that I lost all consciousness. He had sent my body into shock, but through all of that, the only name that I could remember to call on was 'Jesus!' Your grandfather was killing me. My heart beat was fading and my breathing had near stopped, but again I can remember calling on 'Jesus!' When he was through ripping me into shreds, he asked me, 'How does it feel to have another asshole to crap out off, Kiser?' Then he spat on me and left both Sylvia and me lying on the floor bleeding to death. I never saw him again that night. When your grandmother finally got back there with help, my poor Sylvia was lying there with a little breath left in her body. They managed to cut you out, and your poor beloved mother withered into a deep sleep never to be awakened again. I loved Sylvia so much may she forever rest in peace. I just couldn't let her go, I tried replacing her with a Sylvia of my own, but it appears that God said, 'Not so!'"

"As they cleaned you up and I saw that you were well, your grandmother told me that I'd better leave, because the old man would soon return. I struggled to my feet and made my way through the woods. I thanked God for it not being a cold night because I curled up into a ball and slept unconsciously for what felt like hours. I was awakened by the sounds of laughter piercing my ears. It was the devil, he had found me. He told me that they would bury his daughter whom I had destroyed. Then he threatened to bury me and you if I ever ventured near. To my surprise he grabbed me and I pulled up a twig and stuck him in his left eye. As he fell to the ground holding his face, I ran and I didn't stop running until I had grown into what I am now known to be, a true Kiser man."

John stepped from behind the tree which couldn't hold him back anymore. "Kiser, Kiser, you son-of-a-bitch! How could you keep all this to yourself all these years? Do you know what you have done? My mom died looking for her father! How the hell could you do this, and Sylvia, what about Sylvia? So, you named your child after my mother's mama? You are sick! So, Sylvia, my Sylvia is really my blood! I'm going to kill you Kiser, if it's the last thing that I do on this earth! This is so messed up! I can't believe this crap right here today. My insides are boiling over! So, you are my damn granddad? This all has to be a dream!"

Kiser was still in shock, not knowing that someone had actually heard his confession after all of these years. What shocked him most that it was John, whom he didn't realize was back home. It was also the only part of Sylvia, the only person that had ever loved him that he had left to look at and see a resemblance of her. John had his grandmother's eyes and her cheekbones. John had a place in Kiser's heart.

"How could you let all of this happen?" John asked. "I wish that I was killed during the war. Anything would have been better than coming home to find out all of this. Does anyone know who you really are? Is this the reason why you have hated my father all of these years?" John pulled out his pistol and held it to Kiser's head, "You have been to hell and back, why don't I just blow your brains out and take you out of your misery old man! You've screwed up my whole life because you were a punk back in the day! How could you do this to us! Does Sylvia know where she got her name? As a little girl she asked me, if I thought that you hadn't given her a name from the Bible like you had done your other children, because you didn't love her the same. I had told her that her name was full of the anointing and that your love for her was the same. Man, so me and Sylvia are blood! Losing my mom was one thing, but taking the other woman that I love more than I love myself away from me is pure vicious!"

"Sylvia is not your blood! Sylvia is not my child! Sylvia was given to me by God!" After saying this, Kiser walked away.

Chapter 20

"George Kiser was a good kid growing up. But somehow as he aged, some thought that he'd lost his way. I watched Kiser spring from a seed and grow into a plant. I watched the plant bring forth fruit which transformed from unripe to ripe. Once harvested and fully grown, Kiser's sweetness diminished into sour, not to be liked anymore. It seemed like no one cared to know why. I sat back and watched for myself and saw the Devil take over what had once belonged to God." Mr. Tyson explained.

"You knew all of this, all of this that John has told us today?" asked Sylvia.

"Yes, my child, but it was never my place to tell you or anybody else. I tried to do all that I could to help you from afar. I'm old and wise. I've seen enough and been through enough to believe within my heart that the battle is not yours, it's the Lord's! Kiser is a very sick man. He lost it when his Sylvia died. Not you, but Doris's mother. As Doris came into this world, he watched the love of his life die at the same time. It was more than one man could take and he had been hurt by the old man. This was an old man that many had feared. So when word got out that he had lost an eye because of George Kiser, everyone began to fear Kiser more than anyone else. The people didn't know about what happened that hellacious

133

night when Doris was born. The story that was told is that Sylvia had died giving birth due to the baby being breech. They told people that Sylvia had never told a soul who she was knocked up for. The Kiser boys told people that George had beaten the old man for stealing their liquor, which caused him the loss of his eye. After all those stories fell in place, that's what the people believed and day to day life went on." Mr. Tyson had continued on. "I sat back and watched a good man lose his mind. For years George operated his farm and seemed at peace. Then one day he came home with some little skinny gal named Mary. I had never seen a woman near Kiser until he brought home Mary. So I asked him when I saw him again about the skinny old gal, and Kiser told me that she was the one he was waiting for. I asked him why her, and Kiser answered me and said because I was waiting for Mary. I had to have me a Mary."

"He had to have any girl named Mary. Is that what he meant?" I asked.

"As I watched as years went by, I believe that he married her because she was Mary and not for any other reason other than that. He never showed her too much affection; he just had a gal around. Before Mary got pregnant, she would be out there sloping hogs with Kiser. I can remember her out there behind that stink mange mule plowing the fields. Kiser didn't treat her too much like a lady. Kiser was stiff and quiet. To most, he was a stranger with a name. He didn't deal too much with outsiders and he treated his family the same. After leaving his father's place, I can't recall any of them coming over to spend time with him. Kiser preferred being to himself, and I believe that he was afraid of his own mind. How many times can you remember his folks coming around there? Thought so!"

"So, after Paul was born, did Kiser change?" I asked.

"No, Kiser remained the same. He continued to walk around digging in his behind. That's another thing; people always wondered why George dug in his butt so much! He continued to act cold toward the world, but Mary was now happy because she finally had someone to love. Mary stayed in that house and had two more babies, Joseph and Sarah. After realizing that Sarah was messed up, I don't believe Kiser wanted to touch her between the hips again. He started spending longer hours in the field. He would drive down the road every night and sit in a dirt road in the woods by himself for hours and drink, and then sleep. He began to do this every night and he stayed out for hours. I knew that he was trying to connect with Sylvia cause he went out at night like clockwork. After eating dinner, he would storm out of the house and jump into his old Chevy. I believe it was this time of night when he was tired and alone with a little help from the liquor, that his Sylvia would come and visit him. Kiser would pull back into the yard very slowly as if he had seen a ghost. He would sit every night for about another ten minutes before going inside as if he was trying to make peace with what he had just done."

"I still can't believe that he named me Sylvia after Doris's mother." I said

"He did. I believe that Sylvia still visits him from time to time. I bet that it was Sylvia that made him finally confess today at the grave. Sylvia wanted the truth told and only Kiser could tell it. Everyone else that witnessed what happened that night is dead and gone. Then the Lord made it possible for John to be right there and hear it all from the horse's mouth, so nobody ended up being the jackass or had to listen to the jackass!"

"Do you really believe that Mr. Tyson?" I asked.

"Sugar, I've been around here long enough to be able to tell you anything you want to hear. If I should die now, I'd be at peace. My only fear was what would become of you in all this mess. But John is home now; he'll take care of you. I done sit around here and grew old minding everybody else's business. I should've been trying to get me some pussycat! Now they say I got worms, ain't that some crap!"

"Mr. Tyson, you mentioned Paul, Joseph, and Sarah. How were things when I was born?" I had to ask.

"Gal, everybody in this neck of the woods thought that thing was going to hit the fan! While Kiser been going out at night, Young Pastor been stepping in from time to time. I knew it was trouble from the start, cause he didn't ever love that black skinny gal. I sat across this street and watched Pastor Baker put a baby in Mary. He just been a stroking over yonder! He just a stroking and Mary laying up under him just a tarrying. One night Mary cried Jesus so loud that I thought Kiser was going to hear them and find them hitched together, but no, they been some lucky jokers. From that night on, I say that I was going to watch them dogs! Hell, I had no t.v. like them white folks across town, so I watched them dogs and alerted them if I saw Kiser coming before his usual time. That's right, if I even thought I saw Kiser coming down the road and Pastor was in there taking care of business, I would howl just like a coyote."

"Mr. Tyson!" I said.

"Yes, Mary was big and pregnant when she carried you. She swelled up quite a bit. Kiser did make her a walking stick so that she could get around. Mary glowed like never before. It alarmed us how Kiser assisted Mary throughout this pregnancy when he had paid her no attention with the rest. I knew that Kiser had lost it, but this was true confirmation. Why was he being so helpful with this child and not the others? It puzzled me, because I was still waiting on this mess to hit the fan! While Mary was pregnant, Pastor Baker hadn't shown his face around Kiser's farm. That fool didn't even come by for Sunday dinner after church during these months. Kiser had to have picked up on something. But after you were born and he called you Sylvia, I had a dream. The Lord revealed to me that Kiser found a Mary in hopes that God would somehow send him back Sylvia. I then realized that this never hit the fan because in Kiser's mind, he knew that he had not touched Mary, so this child was conceived immaculately by God himself, and her name was to be Sylvia. On the day of your birth, Mary told me that Kiser had told her that on your sixteenth birthday you would become his. See, Mary never knew about the first Sylvia. Sylvia died when she was sixteen, and of course she died on the day of Doris's birth. Then Mary gave birth to you on the same day, just years later. So you and Doris have the same birthday, and Kiser didn't see that as any coincidence. That screwed Kiser up even more!"

"I can't take anymore of this today Mr. Tyson, but I do want to hear more. I have to hear more. I've sat up in that tree trying to figure out this stuff all by myself for years and I couldn't make any sense of it. I thank you for looking out for me all these years. I can remember all of the times you've come over to help me. That's why I believe every word that you have said. You have kept me together when I was falling apart. I don't know what I would have done without you Mr. Tyson! You have been the closest image that I have had as a father figure. I've learned a lot from you throughout the years. If it wasn't for you, Kiser would be barely making it. As a kid, I watched you run your operations and all I did was tweak things a little and made it mine. I wouldn't have known a thing about bootlegging; because Kiser sure didn't know anything about the still or the shine. That reminds me, I got to go. There's one last dollar to be made."

I wasn't making another drop of shine for Kiser. I needed to get my money. I had listened to Paul and had saved up a nice nest egg of cash, stashing a little here and a little there for over a year. I was saving it for the day when he would write and tell me that it was time for Sarah and me to flee. The last I heard from Paul he said the same as the last few letters, "Now isn't a good time." I couldn't wait to tell him about the Kiser mystery. The two of us had wondered for so many years, what could have messed Kiser up so bad and made him such an evil man. I needed to tell him about the night when Kiser was raped and beaten badly. He needs to know that Kiser wasn't always as strong as the father he knows. I now believe that Kiser saw Paul's weakness and was reminded of himself and did to him what was done to him hoping to make him stronger. Now I had to pray that Paul was still okay and that I would receive a letter from him soon.

Thank God John was home now and we were getting married. While I was talking to old Mr. Tyson, John and Mr. Jones was over there fussing with Mr. Kiser. I was hoping that no blood would be shed. John had told me before going over there that if Kiser had to be put down, he was going to put him down and get rid of the evidence. John was still having a very difficult time with the details he had overheard today. He had shared it with me, his daddy and I shared it with Mr. Tyson. I believed that it affected me as much as it affected John. I knew from what we all had just learned that I could never let John find out about Mr. Kiser entering me. Just the thought of all Kiser had been through and the fact that he had put pretty much everyone in his house through the same hell that he experienced and even more, all except for Mary. I didn't believe that John would want me if he found out how many times I was forced to lay with Kiser. He always told me that I was strong, and I was scared that he would think that I wanted Kiser in some way. I knew for sure that he would kill him the same day he found out, so it was best that I take my secret to the grave. Thank God I never told Mr. Tyson.

I was so glad that John told me to stay over at Mr. Tyson's place while he and his dad handled Kiser. John was going to make him understand that both Sarah and I were leaving his house, me tonight and Sarah when we had everything situated for her. My heart had fallen in love with John all over again. He was such a protector. I knew Kiser hated Mr. Jones being on his property, but his overheard soul confession today had weakened him in so many ways. He was hurt, but yet ashamed. This had been a Kiser's secret for as long as this day had happened. And yet, he was the one that spilled the beans.

John told me not to worry and that I wouldn't be staying another night under Kiser's roof. He said that I would sleep in the house with Mr. Jones and he would sleep out in the barn in the hay loft if that would make the people of Deer Island more at ease. For some reason, people had babies out of wedlock. Many had babies for other people's husbands, but if you were shacking up with someone, everyone in Deer Island put your name on the roll for Hell. John said that he was going to marry me as soon as we could find a pastor who would. The thought of Pastor Baker marrying me and John made me sick in the stomach. There was so much that John didn't know and so much that I had to tell him, but when. For now I just wanted to leave Kiser's house. I slept under that roof since the day that I was born there, but now my John had came to set me free. I didn't know if to thank John or to thank God. I had prayed to God many nights to save me, especially those nights when Kiser had laid on top of me. I had never asked John to save me, and it seemed like he was my Savior! I had read the Bible forward and backward and did understand that God had spared John's life and sent him back here to save mine. Even though I had sinned, I knew that I was rooted in Christ. I spoke to God before I started my day, always, and I knew that he forgave me of my sins.

I was so glad when I found all of my cash. Thanks to advice from Paul, I stashed a couple of hundred dollars away. I buried them in several places near the still, in glass mason jars underground. This could help us a great deal, but I'm pretty sure that John came back here with some money. What he didn't have, Mr. Jones had plenty. I wasn't handing over my money just yet. My mind had ventured back to John and all of his learned new tricks he displayed earlier; yeah the ones that made me feel so good. The man had touched me in spots that I only thought Peter could touch as he came dragging out of my cootie. I needed to save my dollars for hard times, in case times of trouble arise. I didn't raise no fool, cause I sure damn raised my damn self! I took my money, then climbed my tree for what I hoped was my last time climbing.

Chapter 21

9 Months Later

We had a shotgun wedding a week after John returned. Luckily for all of us, Kiser let me pack my stuff that night and walk out of his house without a fight. Pastor Baker did marry John and me right there in Mr. Jones' front yard. I didn't want to go inside his church. Pastor looked in my eyes as if he saw nothing on my special day. I watched his every move to see if he would show any emotions, but that old dirty hypocrite acted as if I was just any girl from his congregation. I could tell by the look in my mother's eyes that she loved this man. What a shame for a woman to live with the devil all these years, while being in love with another devil, just one that was familiar with God's word. But even I knew that the Devil was casted out of heaven, so I'm sure he knew Jesus pretty well. I assumed that my mother was a she-devil herself, as she began to cry throughout our vows. This woman never failed to amaze me. Why was she crying? She never cried or helped me any of those nights when her husband would climb on top of me and stick his shriveled up wee-wee inside of me. I was at the verge of hating her, only my relationship that I had with Jesus prevented me from doing so. If only Paul could've been there.

We lived with Mr. Jones while John worked day and night building our house by hand. John would go pick Peter up every day after he got in from school, and Peter would help John as much as his little hands could. He loved being around us, but we knew that after a couple of hours, John had to return him home. He was such a great kid. Well they say, "God knows best."

But little that I knew, we were going to have another one. Who would have thought that on the day of John's arrival, that he would put a baby in me? Yes, I was already married when I found out that I was knocked up again. I was so happy to be pregnant. I knew that only God had fixed it where I didn't ever get pregnant by Kiser. For years I had wondered if my punishment for having Peter without being married was that he would be the only baby that I would give birth to. It saddened me when I thought about it, until the day I discovered that I was pregnant. I didn't know until I felt something that felt like butterflies flying around in my stomach. For days I thought that I had the worst case of gas. I had eaten a half of box of baking soda, trying to free the gas, then I felt the kick. That's when I knew a baby was in there.

Lord, I had pushed all night long to get this boy here. Luke was a nice size, not as big as Peter was though. He looked like he was born tough, looked just like his daddy from day one. I couldn't believe it, but it helped me to understand how the Holy Ghost worked. I had never thought days like this would come, but it was all in God's plans for me. Through it all, I kept trusting and believing that He was going to make a way out of no way for me. As I looked in Luke Jones' eyes I said, "Thank you, Jesus."

John held Luke for a long time. He said that he had dreamed of this moment many nights when it looked like the sky was going to fall on him, as he looked into the clouds. John had shared many war stories with me. His time away was totally different from any day he would have had right here on Deer Island. John had experienced a lot and had killed many for his country. As he drunk my shine day after day, I imagined that he was trying to wash away old memories that dangled in his brain.

John drunk like a fish and I never felt safe leaving Luke with him alone while I took care of my responsibilities. John was a good man, but I could see that he was troubled. Being away in that war had done something to him. He would come in at night smelling of alcohol. Most times, he would find me in the kitchen preparing dinner or putting away the day's harvest. He would come up behind me, pressing himself against me and grind his manly parts everywhere but inside me. If my clothes and underpants weren't between us, I believe he would indeed put it in me right there in the kitchen. I felt like this was his way of saying, "Sylvia, I love you." After that he would sit down at the table and we would talk. We would talk about our day, and our conversation always ended with us talking about our first born, Peter.

Peter loved his new little brother. I was so glad that after all these years he still knew that we were his birth parents but God had placed his other parents in his life until we were able to be better parents. He enjoyed coming over to spend time with Luke and insisted on being the best big brother anyone could ever have. The Riley's had done such a lovely job raising our son, and I only prayed that I could do the same with Luke. John always took Peter back home. He said that he didn't want to kill anybody for messing with his boy. This entire time, I was praying for God to take all of that killing out of John's spirit. I wanted him to protect us, but I heard him talk about wanting to kill somebody or something every day. It didn't help at all when he would go into the back yard and just start shooting, "Pow, pow, pow." That was my John. Now that I knew the truth about Kiser, I often wondered how John got his name. His name was too, from the Bible.

One night while lying in bed nursing Luke, John came in drunk as a skunk. He pulled Luke from my breast and said, "It's my turn to suck on mommy's titties. You've been pulling on them suckers all day."

I said, "John, you have lost your mind, bring my baby back here."

John looked at me and said, "You better take care of your man, cause he's hungry. Your man has been pulling on himself all week, and he could've been with a freak who knew what to do with it. So you better handle your business."

I looked at Luke and he looked as if he was falling asleep. I couldn't believe what John said, but I had been around my shine long enough to know that it made all men speak the truth. John got on me and started sucking the milk right out of my breast. He was slobbering all over me. My thighs were getting wet as he did this and my thick hairs was sticking together all bonded by my natural juices. My nipples got much larger than I had ever seen them. What looked liked raisins now looked like prunes. My teeth were rattling from the pain of his sucks, but my bottom was turning from the feel of his touch. I began to feel drunk and I had nothing to drink. Was it a high that I could only get from him?

John inserted his fingers inside of me, first one, then two, I couldn't believe when he pushed in four. I said, "John, not in front of Luke."

"He's a baby, he doesn't know, but before I'm through I'm making another baby right inside of you." John said.

John threw both of my legs up and back. If I didn't know any better I would have thought we made history. John stayed on me for what seemed like hours. I didn't know that I could bounce like that, but with John I was always finding out something I never even imagined. One night he made me into a pretzel and did something with his tongue that I had only seen him do with a piece of oxtail. Lord have mercy on me, and I thought the Holy Ghost was something. It use to amaze me when I saw people with the Holy Ghost run up and down the church jumping around and screaming out loud. Now my husband had me speaking in tongues and climbing the wall. I looked over at Luke and mumbled these words, "You ain't ever going in the Army, if the Army going to make somebody turn into this." Then I laid back and finished enjoying the ride. A ride that took me to the north brought me back to the south and went to the east and west in between stops. I looked up at John and John spoke these words, "I took you around the world didn't I?" I didn't answer, but I wondered how John had known that.

Chapter 22

Who would have known that what was going to come out of Mr. Tyson's mouth was going to make me pass out? I saw him running through the corn field calling my name, but what could it be? He knew that I was knocked up again and couldn't run to meet him so, what was it?

"Sylvia, Sylvia, Mary's dead. She fell dead under the Pastor!" Mr. Tyson yelled.

When they woke me, Mr. Tyson had to tell me again. This time Mr. Jones and John held me up, fearing I had already put the baby in danger. I said, "What, my mother is dead, dead as in not ever coming back?"

"Yeah, I saw when Pastor got there. He went inside and I didn't see when he came out. Joseph ran over to get me. He said something but all I understood was dead. I don't know why Pastor Baker sent him to be the messenger, knowing good and well that sucker can't talk. It took me twenty minutes to make out what the damn boy was telling me. So I went over there and Pastor Baker was dressed sitting on side of the bed with his hands on Mary. He said that she had a heart attack." Mr. Tyson explained.

149

"A heart attack, mama?" I asked.

"Yep. Pastor was a slick one. He and Mary were fully dressed before he called the boy inside the room. He knew that Joseph was half slow for being almost thirty years old. He told Joseph to get some help. After I got there and confirmed that there was no sign of life, I told the old fool boy to run and find Kiser and I stayed and talked to Pastor Baker."

"You talked to that Bastard?" I asked.

"Yes, somebody has to tell the story so we needed to discuss what story was going to be told. Pastor told me how she looked into his eyes in the middle of his stroke and she took one last big breath. He said she died that easy, not a sign of pain. The story that we'll tell is that she called the church because she was having chest pains and knew that Kiser was too far to be found. The Pastor told her that he would drive over there, because she sounded as if she was in a lot of pain. If he couldn't find Kiser then he would take his member to the hospital himself. When he arrived and knocked to the door, his knock was unanswered. So he walked in and began calling Mary's name. There was no answer. He found himself to her bedroom after checking behind the other doors and he found Mary lying there, dead."

"Who is going to believe that?" Sylvia asked.

"We don't care who believe it, but that is the story. Mary is dead now, let God be the judge of her." said Mr. Tyson.

"My mama is dead. My mama is dead. She died peacefully because she died with the only person that she ever truly loved. I hope that she burns in hell. Who is going in there to tell Sarah? Thank God we took her from that hell hole months ago."

"Y'all handle that. I need to get back over there before Kiser gets there." said Mr. Tyson.

I couldn't accept this right here. I needed to see her for myself. "John, take me to my mother. I'll deal with Sarah later." We left Luke with his grandfather. When I got to the house that I use to call my own, I walked through and went straight to my mama. To my surprise, Pastor Baker was no longer there. Joseph told him to leave, said it wasn't a good idea for his dad to find him there. Joseph had told Mr. Tyson that no one was going to believe that story they came up with. Joseph knew better than anybody that his daddy was crazy. He also knew that he was the only one that would be in this house with him now, since everyone else was gone. So Joseph also had to look out for his best interest. He didn't want Kiser snapping in there with him alone. Joseph told Kiser when he found him sitting in his Chevy down that same dirt road he liked, that he found his mother lying on the floor and that he picked her up and put her into their bed. He told Kiser to come home now, because he didn't think that Mary had any breath in her body.

Kiser just stared at him and didn't say a word. Joseph said, "C-C-C-C-C-ome on." Then Joseph took off running back to Kiser's farm. Kiser sat there, finished his shine, and placed his head on his steering wheel. He cried, but his tears were not for Mary, they were tears that he continued to shed for his dear precious Sylvia. Kiser's love for Sylvia had not died after all of these years. He felt her presence deep in these woods and he heard her voice when she would speak to him. Kiser lifted his head and said, "Sylvia, I believe Mary is dead now. I have to go and make peace. I don't believe that you'll ever meet her, cause her soul does not belong in heaven. Thank you for listening to me talk about her all these years, but now this too shall pass. Watch over your grandson John and continue to protect them from all harm and danger. He is all we got. I look into that boy's eyes and I see you. Thank you for sending him back to me." Kiser drove off.

I sat by my mom and stroked her face and arm. Then I got up and told John that I was ready to go home. There was nothing more to be said. I hugged Joseph and told him to keep me informed of our mother's funeral arrangements, and to let me know if he needed me for anything. I stared at my mother and then I felt a kick, followed by another. That's when I remembered, the Lord giveth and he taketh away.

As we were leaving, Kiser drove up. I stopped and looked at him as he moved slowly getting out of his raggy truck. No words were exchanged as John and I continued on our way. Kiser went inside and looked at his wife, a wife that couldn't take the place of his first love, Sylvia. He checked her pulse and felt for a heartbeat. Kiser then pulled her cover back, lifted up her dress, and said, "Just like I thought, the nasty bastard died with no drawers on!"

On the day of the funeral John and I took Sarah by the funeral parlor early that morning to see her mother for the last time. Even though people now knew about Sarah, I didn't think that this was the proper time to bring her out into the world. Being around that many people would startle her. No need for Sarah to have to beat somebody down just cause Mary's dead. I told her that Mary died, but I wasn't sure how much of what I said that she understood. Mary looked good lying in her cheap casket. She looked like she was sleeping. Kiser didn't pay for the best, but she was lucky he didn't put her behind in a wooden box and said the hell with her.

Sarah looked at her mother, and then looked back at me. Then she spoke, "More." It was then that I knew she understood something and I was glad that I brought her medicine along with me. So, I lit one up and we both took a long drag. I took one and let Sarah have the rest, only because of this baby I was carrying. After living with my siblings, I prayed that all of my kids would come here normal, because Mary and Kiser produced some mess. As I looked at her, I tried to find some of me in her. I didn't have her eyes, nose, cheekbones, or mouth. If they didn't tell me that they saw the midwife pull me out of her, I would wonder if she was my mama.

Mary's funeral was short, that's the way Kiser wanted it. He told the Pastor that he wanted it to be over before it started. Kiser didn't do the church, but because Mary lived in the church he allowed the funeral to be in the church. Pastor Baker had come down with the flu the night before so one of his deacons was doing the eulogy. What a shame, you know that brought attention to the situation for the people of Deer Island. The talk around here was that the Pastor was too emotional to talk over his mistress. That wife of his tried her best to protect her husband. She spoke of how he vomited all night long and had it coming from both ends most of the night. She must have loved that man, because I wasn't surprised if he wasn't at one of his other mistresses' house while the funeral was going on. If I had to go through that, I'd rather be by myself.

Kiser didn't shed a tear at the funeral. Joseph and Mary's siblings were the only people crying. I didn't know if Joseph was crying because his mother's death hurt him so badly or if he was crying because he was the only person living with Kiser now. I didn't care really. My eyes were on Paul since he walked in the church. Who told him about Mary's passing? Who knew how to get in touch with him? The whole time I was worrying about Paul and how this was going to affect him whenever he found out that his mother was dead, and he knew. I was keeping my eyes on him because he wasn't getting away this day without answering some questions. Paul looked good. Someone came and whispered something in his ear and he whispered back. Then he was led into the pulpit. Why were all the pastors and deacons shaking Paul's hand? Before the closing was said, the deacon asked, "Rev. Paul Kiser, would you like to say a few words?" The whole congregation's mouths fell wide open.

Paul said, "No Deacon, not today. My heart is heavy."

Paul is a Pastor. When did he do all of that? I thought that God had to call you. This boy had my chest palpitating so hard I almost said out loud, "John get up off of me and give my heart a break." I was so glad that I realized where I was and what was really happening. Paul and I had to talk. My brother done left Deer Island and bumped his head. He was sitting up there in what looked to me a five piece suit. It looked like he should have sent for me and Sarah a long time ago. He looked like he was doing well to me.

All of a sudden I started fuming, letting these baby hormones get the best of me as the old lady would tell me. I thought about the promises Paul had made me before he left. Suppose John wasn't

154

back yet. What if I didn't discover something that would make Sarah calm down? Paul was being selfish; he had left us and never looked back, until now. John must have felt some tension as I sat beside him. He reached over and squeezed my hand. "Everything is going to be alright. You don't have to worry about nothing." John said.

After Mary was placed six feet underground, it was then Paul came over and hugged me. As he held me, tears finally ran down his face. When I hugged him back, his tears turned into big uncontrollable sobs. "I love you Sylvia and I missed you all so much. How is Sarah? Please tell me that she is alright."

"Paul, how did you find out that Mary was dead?" I asked.

"Mr. Tyson told me. He has kept me up these past couple of years." Paul said.

"But how?" I asked.

"I always made sure that he had a phone number where I was staying in case of emergencies like this. He told me when John came home, about the wedding, and when you took Sarah to live with you." Paul explained.

"Why didn't you send me a contact number? You even stopped writing me. I thought that Mr. Tyson and I were cool. He kept this from me. I was worried sick about you and he knew this."

"I told him to always keep my numbers a secret. All of my numbers belonged to someone else. I didn't want to receive multiple calls on someone else's line. Like I said, I sent the number to him for emergencies only. That was the only time that he called me, when mama died. I called him about every three months to check on you guys. I stopped writing, because I was trying to find myself. I needed to place everyone else's needs aside and search myself. In my searching is when I heard the call from the Lord. Jesus told me so clearly one day, 'Paul, you cannot let your past identify who you are. I took you away from all of your troubles so that your future could be rich. You are your father's son, but you are not of your father. Forgive him and allow my will to be done.' God told me that I was to minister to his people and preach the gospel. I yielded to His call and here I am today."

I don't know why I did it, but I slapped Paul right in the face. I guess I just had to hit somebody, and his behind deserved it. Everyone in the cemetery looked over at us. I looked back at them and asked, "You want some?" I bet they turned their heads then and went on with their gossip. Boy, was I glad that my name was no longer a Kiser, because it seemed as though that was the name of the devil, as I made my way back to John's truck. Mary was now resting in peace, but peace was still far from being still.

I looked back at Paul as John drove off and saw the hurt in his eyes. There was so much confusion within him. Before we got too far away, I did the next best thing that I could do and I blew Paul a kiss. He needed to know that I cared about him. I could really see the sissy in him and wondered how he was allowed to be in somebody's pulpit with that spirit that lived deep within him. He was so soft and clean cut. I'd wondered whose wife was he in that big city in Georgia. I hoped that he would take care of himself. Men like him got killed for looking at another man the wrong way. But if he said God got his back like he said God does, then I believe that my brother is going to be alright. If we survived Kiser, we were strong enough to survive whatever the world threw at us.

Those nasty ugly sisters of Mary had followed everyone to Kiser's house. The people came for food and liquor. The Dunlap sisters came for Mary's things. The nerve of these ugly, poor people harassing Kiser on the day he buried his wife. They were all in his face asking for Mary's things. I guess they felt safe in large numbers. When Mary was living, they acted like they were too afraid to visit. It seemed like a few of them wanted to be next in line as the new Mrs. Kiser the way they were pulling on his pants and rubbing against his thighs. Kiser was in a daze, and none of their words were reaching him on this day. As I looked at those ugly heifers, I was so glad. I'd never had to struggle like that. Every time I thought about Kiser being the best thing that ever happened to my mama, my stomach rolled-over and I wanted someone to stick a fork in me.

I went home and put Luke to bed. As I laid in my empty bed, I rubbed my stomach hoping that this baby was a little girl. Then I reminisced on the good times that me and my mama did have and Sarah beating both of our tails brought laughter which was good for my soul. On that night I fell asleep and didn't even worry myself about where John could be. Peace was now still and in my world, that was all that mattered.

Chapter 23

John

I love Sylvia, God knows that I do, but those freaks in the war messed me up. Better yet, I need to go further back in time, those freaks that my father and uncles brought into their beds while I was in there messed me up. They were the reason that I held Sylvia down when she was nine and nearly raped her. She didn't know what I was trying to do to her. After I did it to her the first time, she was fair game after that though. I must have made her feel real good. I still feel sorry for getting her pregnant so young, because it caused her whole childhood to be taken away from her. Kiser not allowing her to go back to school really scared me. I still need to find out who Sylvia's real dad is, because that is still on my mind. All my life I had wondered who Doris's father was, amazingly I found that out. Now I don't know who my wife's father is.

I wanted to see Peter, so I decided to venture on over there. The Riley's were usually home. They were very quiet people. So, I knocked at the door and waited. I saw Patricia coming through the screen door. That woman had a set of hips on her; no one would believe that she had never birthed any babies from between those hips. It made me want to ask her if Melvin, excuse me, I meant Mr. Riley was touching that cat in the right way to make that thing snap, crackle, and pop. Patricia came to the door with her Bible in hand. She opened the door and said that Peter and Melvin were out in the deer stand, and that she didn't know when they would return.

So, I asked Patricia what she was reading. She said that she was reading back over some chapters from the Pastor's last sermon. "Would you mind reading those scriptures aloud in my hearing before I leave?" I said.

"If you really want to listen to me read, I guess I can do that." Patricia said.

Patricia invited me in and we sat to the table in the kitchen. As Patricia was reading, John was watching this older lady's lips while licking his lips. He saw what looked like sweat running between her breasts. After every few words read by Patricia, John would throw in a few words just enough to let Patricia know that he knew the Bible as good as her or even better. The scripture reading sparked discussions from the two. Patricia seemed to be impressed that John was such a Bible scholar. For some odd reason, John blew a kiss at her. The next thing John knew his lips were on Patricia's lips. Patricia pushed John away at first, but she must have realized that she had never felt that way from a kiss, so she looked at him and hoped that he would lean in and do it again. Instead, John said, "I'm sorry, I really should leave and I won't enter your home again, I'll just get Peter and go."

Patricia said, "Don't be sorry, it was nice."

"It was? You look so nice I guess I couldn't help myself." said John.

"Thank you John, no one ever tells me that." Patricia said.

"I don't know why, you are gorgeous, and your hips are so round. Melvin doesn't tell you that? I've always wondered what those jersey cow tits of yours looked like. I was watching you back in the day when all your hair was black."

"No, Melvin doesn't talk to me like that. We don't talk about how we look or how we feel. I guess we've been together so long."

"Let me kiss you again and I want you to tell me if you like it." said John.

"Ok, but make it quick." said Patricia.

John knew that he was going in for the kill, so he checked both doors to make sure that no one was coming. John looked Patricia in her eyes and saw the loneliness hidden there. Peter was probably the only reason why she was happy. John grabbed Patricia and pulled her into him. Patricia didn't resist, so what John did next, led to all of their clothes coming off and John entering her doors. John worked it so good with this older lady that probably hadn't ever been touched in any of those spots besides with a washcloth. John went in her front and back doors, something yet he was unable to do with Sylvia. What a night to remember. So now Patricia would be his Bible study freak partner on Thursday nights, which was also Melvin and Peter's father/son night outings.

After a night like that, John went straight to the hay loft. He still couldn't believe that he had boned Peter's other mother. Patricia was old enough that she could have very well been his mother too. John looked up at the sky and said to himself, "I didn't know aged women was as good as aged wine. Mr. Riley hasn't even been knocking the dust off of that cat. I had to plunge through all sorts of cob webs to reach my final destination.

Old Patty is a tiger and she didn't even know it. With her bad self, quoting scriptures while I was hitting it. Then when I flipped her over and entered her back door, Patty said, "Jesus, remember, you promised to never leave me or forsake me, but I thank ya anyhow."

I felt sorry for what I had done. But with this pregnancy and the stress of the loss of her mother, Sylvia didn't want any sex at all. She had grown huge and unattractive and I loved her still. I would love Sylvia without the sex, kisses, or hugs, because that's not why I fell in love with her in the first place. Patricia and the other freaks were just my way of getting my physical needs met. Those other women didn't have to do anything for me when I knew that they were coming to meet me. I had my man primed and ready to go by my damn self. If it took them too long, I would pull the trigger and shoot the load on myself, empty the barrel if I could. I didn't care. My name was John Jones and all the ladies loved me.

I went into the house early the next morning. Sylvia was in the kitchen waiting for me. "Where did you sleep last night?" Sylvia asked.

"I had a lot on my mind. I knew that you and Luke were tired from such a long day. So instead of coming in bed with you and tossing and turning, I slept in the hay loft. This stuff about Kiser being my grandfather still bothers me. You weren't worried about me were you?" John said.

"Of course I was worried about you. After you brought us home you left, and this is my first time seeing you since then. I meant to call your daddy and ask him if he knew your whereabouts, but I figured I'd wait until sunrise." said Sylvia.

"I'm sorry, it won't happen again." John said.

That evening, John got himself a ripe apple and cut it in half. He stood in the kitchen and rubbed it all over himself. Then he took both halves of apple and placed them in his pockets.

"What are you doing with that apple John?" Sylvia asked.

"I'm going in my tree stand. I use the apple to hide my human scent. The deer will smell the apple and come right to me. I learned in the army to work smart, not hard. Last time I did this, I shot three deer right in the head. I'm a Jones, which makes me a bad man. Everybody trying to keep up with the Joneses, but they don't even know how we do what we do. One day I'll take Peter up in my deer stand and let him see how a real man kills a deer."

"What do you mean by that? Peter hunts with a real man now, Mr. Riley." Sylvia said.

"Whatever!" said John.

"What is that supposed to mean?" Sylvia asked.

"Woman, there aren't too many real men around here. I can only name a few. They act like they are half dead to me. I can name about ten that couldn't get up for their wives in a rainstorm."

"You sure have changed in the last year. I've been listening to you talk that same yang-yang for a while. Are you trying to tell me something? You going to mess around and the next batch of shine that I make for you is going to make that dip stick of yours fall off." Sylvia said.

"You called my penis a dip stick, well I have never."

"You talk about it like you have dipped it in gold or something finer all of the time. After I get this here baby out of me I will be going down there to that juke joint with you. I've been to hell and back while you were gone. There's still a lot that you don't know that went on while you were gone, and some of it I'll never care to tell you." Sylvia said.

"Tell me what?"

"All I'm saying is that I want a little more respect around here. I'm taking care of Luke, Sarah, you and your daddy. I work hard. Ran the still for years and came over here and now you and your daddy got me running the still for y'all. All I'm asking you to do is respect me." Sylvia said.

"Respect, woman, I respected you by coming back and marrying your big butt. You know how I feel about you. I'll never love another or be with another as long as I shall live. You're the only jelly for my beans. You hear me? You don't have to ever worry about me. I just like to talk a lot of trash. It makes me feel good. Now, if all hearts are cleared, get in there and take them clothes off. Big Daddy is home and he wants something tasty to eat."

"John, you don't have to be nasty all of the time you know." Sylvia said.

"I know baby. I'll just be nasty some of the times, and just with you baby. Now let me see if you remembered how to back it up for me. Beep-Beep-Beep! You are getting wide back there. I'm going to have to put a sign on you in a minute, wide load."

"I love you too, John. When we're done, please go and see if it's alright for Peter to come over. I miss him." Sylvia said.

"It would be my pleasure."

Chapter 24

Sylvia

Here I was laid up in the house for two weeks now since Matthew was born. I believed in my heart that this was going to be my little girl right here. When I heard, "It's another boy." I wanted to die. Matthew was a fine baby, just not what I wanted. One night I felt so angry I smoked some of Sarah's medicine. That life everlasting was the key for everything. I felt so good. I didn't care if I had ten Matthews running around in here.

I found out later that smoking that stuff was a big mistake. Later that night after nursing Matthew, his eyes began to roll back into his head. His breathing became heavy and I didn't know what to do. I ran out and got John and Mr. Jones and told them to come in a hurry. Poor Matthew was just laying there and Luke was asleep beside him. He had fallen asleep while I was smoking and was still asleep. John grabbed my baby and placed his tiny body on the floor. John was breathing and blowing into him while pounding on his chest. Oh, how my heart jumped when I heard my baby cry.

Putting two and two together, I guess the herb traveled through my breast milk and Matthew sucked as much as his belly could hold. That belly full was enough to kill him, but God gave him back to me. Oh my, what a lesson learned. One minute I hated him because he was a boy and the next minute I was praying to God, asking him to save my baby boy. I held Matthew for what seemed like eternity, knowing that this episode would probably make me feel as though I owed my entire life to him for as long as I lived. God had a funny way of turning things around without our knowledge.

Poor Luke was also affected by the smoke as I smoked my herb. That's what put him to sleep so soundly, he had never slept like that before. My poor child was knocked out. On this night, I vowed never to smoke life everlasting again. Just as long as I kept some around here for Sarah we would be alright. She didn't need it like she used to. She was free to roam the house and go on the porch, just as long as someone was around to monitor her. She loved watching John and Mr. Jones as they busied themselves around the farm.

Sarah had more freedom here, but she preferred staying in her room most of the time with her door closed. Most times she would close the door behind her when she went inside. I didn't know if it was because she was use to being locked up at Kiser's, or if it was because that's really just how she was going to be regardless of what Kiser had done to her. Now that I think about it, we never had a lock on Sarah's door when she was younger. We just made sure to close it all of the time. Sarah never tried to come out of her room. Maybe she assumed a closed door meant to stay put. I just wished that she could speak her mind. I had taught her how to communicate with me by using pictures. I came up with this idea because I wanted Sarah to have a choice regarding what she wanted to eat. The big blessing was she did come out to use the toilet. No more dumping buckets for me. I was beginning to think that some of the terrible things that she did, she did intentionally. She probably treated us the way she did, because of all the mean evil spirits that she sensed. Life for Sarah was so different here.

When Mr. Tyson heard about my babies, he ran over here. He said that he couldn't take anymore news today. I asked him what other news he had heard.

"Which one do you want first, the ridiculous or the miraculous?" Mr. Tyson asked.

"What? You've got to be kidding me. Deer Island has news like that. I know neither one is bigger than you and your marijuana plants putting us on the map. So, let me hear the ridiculous first."

Mr. Jones said, "Are you sure about that?"

"Let me have it."

"Well, I saw it for myself. Mr. Kiser came home with a new wife. That woman so big and ugly, I know that Kiser is going to have to brown bag that woman to sleep with her. After Sylvia, he must have vowed not to ever get a decent looking woman again. Sylvia was beautiful. These two wives Kiser got could sleep outside with the dogs." Mr. Tyson said.

"Kiser married? Are you sure? Lord have mercy on her."

"It didn't take me long to figure out why he married this heifer. They came in yesterday by themselves. Tonight when Kiser's truck came in, they brought two big meat head boys and a plump girl with them. Those boys were going to be bigger than their mama pretty soon and the girl looked to be the oldest of the three of them. I said to myself, Kiser married that woman for them children she got. He'll make farm hands out of those boys. He told me a while ago that he wanted to find a girl for Joseph. So there you go, Kiser got this heifer for her calves."

"That sure is some ridiculous news right there." Mr. Jones said.

"Okay, it's going to take me some time to digest that one, but go ahead and tell us the miraculous news." Sylvia said.

"After I stopped looking at Kiser's place, I noticed all of the cars at the Riley's place. So I jumped on my bike and pedaled over there. I saw the Pastor's car and several of the deacons' cars. I thought that someone was sick or dead. I barged myself right in their house without saying a word. I was scared. Y'all ain't never going to believe this one right here."

"Just tell us." Sylvia said.

"Or don't tell us and take your nosey behind home. Always minding people's business and don't have a got damn business of your own, since you got old and about to expire." John said.

"Shut up John and leave Mr. Tyson alone. I want to hear the news. You don't see anything on that black and white television in there that's good enough to watch." Sylvia said.

"Yeah, just as long as I'm not talking about you John, let me talk. Well, Sister Riley has found out that at the age of fifty-three she is pregnant. They are all over there anointing her with oil asking God to bless Patricia and Melvin with a biological child of their own. She lost all of her other babies you know. She hasn't been pregnant since a hacket was a hammer and they said tonight she was twenty six when she had her last miscarriage and hadn't been able to get pregnant since. If you go over there now, you bound to catch the Holy Ghost with all that praying they got up in there." Mr. Tyson said.

"Mrs. Riley is going to have a baby. How in the world did that happen?" Sylvia asked.

"Sylvia, the way you have been having them babies over here, you should be the last to ask that question." Mr. Tyson said.

Mr. Jones said, "Don't get excited so fast. The woman was pregnant a lot of times when she was young, but her body couldn't hold the baby. She'll probably lose this one too. I told Melvin years ago that he married spoiled goods. That's why I told all my brothers to big them gals first before they jumped a damn broom."

"Well, while I was over there I heard someone mentioned that this was the longest she had carried a baby so things were looking good. She just didn't seem as happy as an old woman should have been who was finally getting her prayers answered. This was a prayer that I knew she prayed for years, even though she had Peter. Peter has always been an angel for the Rileys, but just like anything else, there is nothing like your own." Mr. Tyson said.

"I wonder when she is going to tell Peter. This will be a big surprise for him. It also can change his life drastically. He loves Luke and Matthew, but he never had to share Mrs. Riley with nobody." Sylvia said.

"Please people, enough with all this bunch of bull! Sylvia do you think that you can get us fifty gallons of shine with the apples by Friday? The big game is being played in the city across the big bridge and I heard that those folks been asking for our shine the last game. There's money to be made out there if Sylvia would get back there and work."

"We don't have any apples. I told you that last week. If you would do your part, maybe we could make some money. How do you expect me to be back in those woods when you can't sit with your own babies for fifteen minutes at a time?" Sylvia said.

"Woman mind your manners out here talking to your husband like that. A Jones man will not be disrespected." Mr. Jones said as he walked off.

"I heard that Doris disrespected you many of times, Mr. Jones. That is your name isn't it? She died disrespecting you." Sylvia said.

Before Sylvia knew it, Mr. Jones and John were in her face. "I'm not afraid of you two. See, when you've been through what I've been through and God brought you through it, there's not a man on this earth that can steal your joy. I went through more pain and suffering than Doris could ever imagine. Just like Doris, I don't have a daddy! Neither one of you were there that day to save me on my sixteenth birthday when I was burned on my foot as I was priming the still. The mush that fell on my foot was so hot that the skin on my foot rolled off, as soon as I touched it, which left this scar that is still here today. All I could do is lay on that rough, hard, gritty ground. I screamed for help. When I thought my help had arrived, to my surprise this man came and made my pain turn into a state of shock. I had forgotten that I had a foot because of his rage. He pushed me down further while ripping at my clothes. He raped me! He poisoned my insides and made me bleed with every stabbing force of his manhood. He took that same manhood and polluted my mouth. I guess that wasn't enough that day, cause he raped me over and over again until I just couldn't hurt anymore. When Doris got shot in the head, she didn't suffer. She was taken out of her misery. Just like me, she couldn't hurt anymore. The same man that hurt Doris was the same man that hurt me." Sylvia said.

"Sylvia, Sylvia, you know who killed my mama?" John asked.

"Just like I thought John, Doris isn't here anymore. She's been dead for a long time. You should have asked who hurt me first, but no you two so hung up on a lady that never did anything for either of you. Doris had a choice when she decided to walk out on y'all that day. She was grown; she didn't need a daddy at that point in her life. She left a good family for the streets and her only excuse was in search of her father; a father that we know now to be Kiser. If she had lived to learn who her father was, I bet she would have wished she had never known." Sylvia said.

"Sylvia, I'm sorry. Why didn't you tell me? I'm going to kill this monster if it's the last thing that I do on this earth. Tell me who did this to you. Who raped you Sylvia? Sylvia, if you don't tell me right now." John said.

"What are you going to do John? I can't be hurt no more. So what are you going to do? You can't do anything because that man that hurt both Doris and me is now dead." Sylvia said

"He's dead, how did he die?" John asked.

"Very similar to Doris, when Doris was shot her brains was splattered all over the place. No one could put it back together. This man's brains did the same, got blown into pieces." Sylvia explained.

"You're not going to tell us who he was, are you?" Mr. Jones asked.

"Nope, after today I'm burying it all." Sylvia said.

John said, "I'm going to find out, but what I want more than anything else Sylvia is for you to give me a girl. Give me a girl that I can love and show her how a little girl is supposed to be loved. I want to give her the love you or my mother never had. I wish that I could take away your pain. This explains why I sometimes feel as though I'm hurting you when we're together. There have been times when you made me feel rejected Sylvia. You made me feel like I was just a ton of moving bricks on you. Then there were times when I could tell that you were feeling me. At those times when I felt rejected by you, were you thinking about him?"

"Yes, and I was ashamed." Sylvia said.

"Never feel ashamed. I just wish that I was the one that blew his brains out. You know that I would protect you from anything in this world. If I had known this was happening to you while I was gone, I would have blown up Deer Island. Now please go get them crying babies, I can't take any more of them boys around here. I need a baby girl, Sylvia!"

Chapter 25

Some people are just like graveyards. They never have anything to give. They are always taking this and that from everybody. I've never wanted to be like that. Ever since I had known, people were trying to keep up with the Joneses. This was way before I became one myself. Now that I was a Jones myself, I was no longer on the outside looking in. I knew just how great things were on the inside for myself. We were living in a big house sitting up on a hill, not too far from another big house, which belonged to Mr. Jones. Mr. Jones' brothers all lived behind us in smaller, but nice houses as well. Our houses sat distant from the main road with our private road enclosed by a gate. Many said that it was this gate that separated the Joneses from all the rest of Deer Island. If something was new to Deer Island, it was a Jones that got it first.

Realizing how we got what we have was a mystery to me for a long time, because most of what we have, they had before I came here. I sat up high in my tree many days while I was bootlegging for Kiser and watched the fancy cars and fancy ladies enter the Jones' gate. As John's playmate as a child, John always came and played on my side of the world. So I had not ventured in until he came back from the war to get me.

177

After making those fifty gallons of shine for John to deliver for the big baseball game downtown that night, I began to slowly see how it was done. As John was loading up the truck he said to me, "Baby, I hope that you put your foot and more in this batch of shine, cause I'm going to give them all of these for nothing."

"You are going to what?"

"You heard me. I don't want one red cent for any of it and I won't take a dime. This will be free of charge for them jokers to try. See these people bought the old people who ran things out. I know that they haven't had the best yet, because they haven't had any of our liquor. What better way to convince a rich man to try your product than to offer it all for free. Once they taste it, they will be hooked. Once they are hooked, guess what? Their friends and business partners are hooked, too." John said.

"So I made all this shine and you are going to take it and just give it all away. How stupid. I know that you know how much money we can get for this stuff. I've never seen somebody just give away everything like y'all do in my life."

"Sylvia, I have no time for this right now. I need you to continue to handle your responsibility in the area of production in our deals, and let me handle the business side of it. Have I allowed you to suffer yet? You never have to leave this house if you don't want to because you have everything that you need right here. I make sure of that. We Joneses do things differently from everyone else. All the lumber that I got to build our house, I didn't have to pay a dime for any of it. My father has been giving the owner of the store fresh produce and other services for free for more than twenty years. They have what I call a partnership of some sort. My uncle the mechanic fixes cars for that dealership across the creek when he's done on the farm, some days for no charge at all. When we want a fine car to drive from time to time, the owner of the car dealership lets us drive one right off his lot. He trusts us, knows that we are good people. We drive it where we need to go and then we take it back, all in one piece. No one knows what we have back here on our property. One hand washes the other, baby. We are blessed because of our giving. If my family is going to prosper because of what I give, I'll give the shirt off my back if I have to." John said.

After that night I have been busy ever since. The orders for my shine were coming in too fast. What John said worked too well. I told him one day that I guess that was a good example of sowing your seeds. He laughed so hard he rolled on the ground. Now, my problem was keeping up. Here I was pregnant again for the fourth time and running a still every day. I needed help. John would take Luke and Matthew with him so that I could work my tail off. If I ever had a tail, I didn't have one anymore.

I have always run my still without help because I didn't want anyone to steal my recipe or see what I did differently. On this day as I was walking out of the house, I looked back and Sarah had walked out behind me. I left her standing on the porch. As I walked farther away, my nerves got the best of me and I turned around to go back. I knew that I wouldn't be able to work in peace, not knowing if Sarah went back into her room or not. When I got to the house, Sarah was sitting on the step. I knew that I couldn't waste much time, so I was thinking fast. That's when it hit me. I got an idea and I hoped that it would work out the way I thought of it.

I grabbed Sarah by her hand and led her in the woods. She remained calm and this was good. She sat on a tree stump and watched me diligently. When it was time to bottle the shine, I brought her over and modeled for her how to fill and top each jug. She caught on quick and was very good at it. The one thing that I noticed was everything had to be exactly right. Sarah started her lines over many times until she thought that they were right, which didn't matter to me. Sarah created perfect lines with the gallon jugs. She had become a pro in a day.

John and Mr. Jones were thrilled when they found out that Sarah was helping me back there. John said that Sarah was slowly coming out of her shell and she was going to surprise us one day with all of her hidden talents. After Sarah had finished filling the jugs, she loaded the truck for John as well. John wanted to pay Sarah in some way for all of her hard work. So he told me that he was going to buy her a whole new wardrobe, which was exactly what she needed. After this baby gets here, I was determined that I was going to lose these extra eighty pounds I had gained in the past few years just sitting around here barefoot and pregnant. Then I too was getting a new wardrobe. Mr. Tyson told me that I needed to start eating standing up so that my food could get to my legs. He said that I was starting to look like a white potato with legs. Right now, looking like whatever wasn't my main concern. I was praying night and day for this baby to be a little girl.

While I was feeding my babies there was a knock at the door that scared me half to death. It was very usual for someone to knock at our door, because we didn't have unexpected guests to pop up often. I dragged to the door and to my surprise it was Melvin Riley and Pastor Baker. Mr. Riley I wanted to let in, but Pastor Baker, he was another story. Pastor Baker could have laid flat at my door like a door mat and let me just walk all over him. That would have made me happy. I wondered for a minute what their purpose for being here could've been before letting them in.

"Good evening men, what brings y'all by here today?"

"How are you Sylvia? I hope that we didn't stop by at a bad time. How is everyone doing?" Mr. Riley said.

"Everyone is fine. The boys are at the table and John is out there somewhere." Sylvia said.

"Oh yes, I believe that John is on his way in. Peter spotted him picking okras and ran over there to join him. John yelled and told us that he would be over here shortly." Mr. Riley said.

We sat around chit chatting for a few minutes until John was able to join us. Pastor Baker still hadn't spoken a word. I was very curious about their visit. Neither man had ever come by the house, so this visit I knew was serious. John came in and washed his hands, while Peter joined Luke and Matthew at the table in the kitchen. My big butt was already soaking wet from worrying and sitting on this hard plastic that we kept on our good couch to protect it. I was hoping that John would sit somewhere else and not ask me to slide over because the back of my thighs felt like they were stuck to the plastic. I really need to calm down. "Lord, hold my mule." I thought.

"What have we done to deserve this visit this evening?" John asked.

"Well, this is a personal visit. I know that we sit before you as Deacon and Pastor, but right now I believe Pastor Baker wants you both to forget about that." Mr. Riley explained.

John questioned, "Oh, it is? So go ahead and tell us what brings you by."

Mr. Riley sat back in the chair, "The Pastor knows that I know the both of you pretty well. He told me that he needed to come by and talk to Sylvia, and asked if I would be willing to come with him. He felt like whatever it is he needed to discuss would be better digested if someone she was comfortable with was here with him. He has known the both of you since y'all were babies, but he has never had any dealings with either of you. So I'm going to sit back and let him talk if you allow."

"Alrighty, this should be interesting." John smirked.

Looking rather weak, Pastor Baker began, "I thank you both for allowing me into your fine home this evening. I come with great sympathy about what I'm about to disclose to y'all. Sylvia, I first want to extend my condolences to you since losing your mother almost two years ago. I know that you both heard about me losing my wife a few months back. Losing someone that you care about is one of the hardest things a person has to go through here on this earth. This I have learned for myself, but I do know that if a man loses himself and doesn't find his way, then this is much harder on a man than the first."

The Pastor continued, "I'm stepping down from my position at the church. I haven't told anyone this yet except for those in high positions. I'm passing my torch onto Deacon Riley and he will become the new Pastor of Deer Island Baptist Church."

"What does any of this have to do with Sylvia and you having to come to my house? Is it because you are concerned because I attend church and Sylvia does not? If so Pastor, I've been trying since I came back here to get her to go. She was going before I left for the Army and I was surprise that she had stopped. A lot has happened to my Sylvia and I believe that she has lost all faith in God for allowing these things to happen to her, and this is her reason for not coming." John said.

"Shut up John, that is not why I stopped going to church."

Interrupting Sylvia, the Pastor said, "John, I don't know why Sylvia stopped coming to church, but remember what Deacon Riley said to you guys earlier, I am not here as your Pastor. Let me finish. I'm stepping down because I'm sick. My health is failing me. I can no longer be a shepherd over my sheep like the Lord would have me to be. This old flesh is getting tired and there's something I have to do before my soul can rest. I've sinned so many times as we all have. I have fallen short way too many times. I've asked the Lord for forgiveness and know that thou have forgiven me. What I'm about to say right now may change how you both feel about things in Deer Island forever. Sylvia, I am your father."

At that moment the room fell quiet. Deacon Riley stood up and said, "Well I'll be damn, how in the hell did you do that Pastor?" I believe that he was the most shocked person in the room. I figured that the Pastor had already told him what news he was going to bring, but now I saw differently.

"You are Sylvia's father!" John yelled.

"Yes, I am. I am deeply ashamed, not because of what was created but I am because of how she was created. The part that I played in the creation of such a beautiful person was so wrong. I loved Mary and we were seeing each other for a long time. It was something about her desire to be loved that made her good loving hard to resist. I allowed temptation to get the best of me. There were many times that I wanted to reach out to you, but I feared for you and Mary too much to do so. George Kiser was known as one of the cruelest man that ever lived here during our time. It was probably this opinion that made my experiences even more enjoyable. They have always said that a thief continues to steal because of the rush he gets over not getting caught. Even though I kept seeing Mary, I still was afraid of what might happen to the both of you in that house with Kiser if he found out. This was also Mary's fear. I believe that I loved Mary more than I loved my own wife, but knew for sure that I couldn't do anything about the situation. As a Pastor, it would have looked very bad for me to leave my wife for another man's wife. I am a sinner. The sinner within me allowed my flesh to have both my wife and your mother."

John jumped in, "You nasty dog you. How do you preach the word to us about living according to God's words and you were out there committing adultery? I had heard about you and Mrs. Smith, the pie lady, and Ms. Green, but I didn't know about Mary. How could you be Sylvia's father and not be a part of her life, ever? You are such a devil!"

"John, I believe that the Pastor said earlier that he was afraid of Mr. Kiser. I'm not taking up for the Pastor in any way, because I am just as shocked as you are. But let's not judge him. Our judgment day will come and none of us will be the one doing the judging. The Pastor has done what the Lord allows us all to do and that's repent of his sins."

"But he's such a hypocrite. Wait until my father finds this out. He told me about you preachers. He said he wouldn't sit in that church and listen to another man tell him what God has to say because he can hear from God himself. He said that all we are doing is building up the Pastor's kingdom when we give our money to the church. My father says that he has never seen so many poor people give money to the church when they don't have what they need for their damn self. He always said that if those people were smart, that they would sow seeds into the ground and reap a good harvest. Then they could see how God blessed them. He was right!" John slapped the coffee table.

"Sylvia, are you alright? You haven't spoken a word since Pastor Baker told you that he was your father." Mr. Riley asked.

"I don't know if to laugh or cry. Here I am, a grown woman about to birth my fourth child. You married me under the sun, and you wait until now to tell me this. Sick or not Pastor, you should have carried this to your grave. You sat at that dinner table many Sundays eating dinner at our house, and you didn't even speak to me. You wait until you've buried both my mother and your wife to prepare yourself for this day. You are such a coward. Do you want to know why I stopped coming to Deer Island Baptist? I stopped coming because when I looked up at you I saw my eyes, my nose, and my cheekbones. When I saw you hugging your children as you greeted them, I saw more of me in you than I saw of any of those that you hugged. But yet, there was never a hug for me. No one would have known why you were hugging me. I've suffered for years, because I knew that you were my father and I was hurt by the way you treated me, especially since you were a man of God. A man that most looked up to. What hurt me and my brothers even more was knowing that our mother loved you so much and didn't show us much love at all. Her heart belonged to you and she died right under you! Pastor, you are a bad man. I don't need you now, so you can leave. My babies are tired and I have to go and put them to bed. I vow not to ever be the type of mother Mary was to us, and I pray that God would not allow John to be the type of husband that you were to your wife. They should charge you with murder or at least for leaving the scene of an accident. The man that killed my mother with his pipe has come to tell me that he's my father! How am I supposed to react to that? Jesus!"

"With that said Pastor and Deacon, goodnight." John said while motioning them to the door.

Mr. Riley called Peter from the kitchen, where he was enjoying spending time with his younger brothers. Peter looked as if he was also happy to go home with Mr. Riley. He came running and bouncing like he had just won a prize. He stopped and gave both John and me a hug. When Peter got to the door where Mr. Riley was standing, he said, "Mommy Sylvia, when are you coming to see my new little brother? You have to come and see him. He is so cool. God gave him the same face just like Daddy John and Brother Luke. You have to see for yourself. When are you coming?"

"Wow, I was waiting until he got a little older, but I'll come see him sooner just for you sweetie. What is his name again?"

"His name is Mark."

"Mark, I see. Who gave him that name?"

Mr. Riley spoke up this time, "Patricia said that he couldn't have any other name but Mark. She said that the Gospel of Mark is the second book in the New Testament and Mark was her second child in a new era. She also said that the author of the Book of Mark was Mark the Evangelist, the companion of Peter. With Peter being his brother, she felt this name was most fitting."

"Okay, that's pretty deep. Well, it's been a long evening. Take Peter home so that he can get some rest."

While John closed the door, Sylvia thought to herself. Mark has the same face as John and Luke. Paul told me that I had the same face as Pastor Baker. I will see this child tomorrow. How can this be? Maybe Peter means something else. If I don't go tomorrow, I'll get there someday. The hell with someday or tomorrow, I'm going today!

Chapter 26

I was broken and God put me back together. He delivered me from all of my pain and made me strong. I am no longer weak. There were times in my past when I felt like taking my own life, but something told me not to give up on God. God said, "I'll give you the strength that you need to run this race until the end, Sylvia." He said it, but as I walked through this corn field trying to take a shortcut, I didn't believe it.

I should have called first, but I didn't. Mr. Riley had heard my son Peter begging me to come over and see this baby, and he didn't say anything about not coming. As I looked through their door, I saw them gathering things together. It looked like I had come at a bad time. I didn't see Peter, but Mrs. Riley was holding her newborn. From what I could hear, it sounded as though they were arguing about something. I decided that it was best for me to leave and come back. No need to stir in mess and make it smell stinker.

As soon as I placed one foot down the step I heard, "Even my little boy can see that Patricia! Who are you trying to fool, me or you?" yelled Mr. Riley.

"I'm not trying to fool anybody. I am married to you, we sleep together, and this here is your child!" screamed Patricia.

"You know what the Bible says right? A little child should lead them. I have looked into Mark's face time and time again trying to find me in him. It wasn't until tonight when little Peter said to Sylvia, 'Mark, Daddy John and Brother Luke have the same face,' that I finally made the connection. I came back here and looked into his eyes for confirmation, and what the child saw was so. As a grown man I asked myself how this can be, and if it is so, when?"

"Melvin, I don't know what you are talking about. Right now we should be celebrating. You've always wanted to be a Pastor and many times we have talked about moving so that you could make this a reality. Look how God has blessed us. We don't even have to leave Deer Island. He made a way out of no way just for you. Don't let what Peter said this evening put doubt in your mind. This is the child that we have prayed and prayed for. When I look at Mark, all I see is our big blessing in a little package. He has my dimples and lips. If you look hard enough, you can see that he has your forehead. You know what the old folks say about babies anyway. 'You can't tell who they really look like until they are much older, and by that time you have probably fed them til they look like ya by then.'" Patricia said.

"Is that right? I hear you talking Patricia, but the truth shall set you free! Let me put a few more things in my bag, and I'm out of here for a few days. I'm going to drive to Georgia and stay with my brother for a couple days before Sunday. I need to clear my head and get myself together for the biggest day in my life. I also need to pray for Pastor Baker. It's a shame how after all these years, he hasn't stopped with this nonsense of sleeping with different women. He may have stopped now, and only because he is half dead and has one foot in the grave. It's been seventeen years since I caught that cheating hypocrite in my house, and he begged me for years not to say anything to his church members. I forgave the both of you like a fool after y'all shared such a touching story with me that I now know to be a lie. I can't believe I listened to that punk when he told me that the Lord said that he was to be with you, and through him you would become fruitful and be able to multiply. As I pray for him, I have to ask God to touch all of those that Pastor Baker has touched in his special way, because after John mentioned a few other ladies tonight that Pastor Baker had relations with, I then realized something quite interesting. I also sat up straight in my chair because, I thought he was going to call your name as well. So I guess he didn't hear about you. All of the ladies that John mentioned are now dead along with their spouses, except for Kiser. Pastor Baker is now sick and he hasn't told anybody what kind of sickness he has. Kiser and Mary didn't seem to be affectionate for years before she died, and Mary shared with us during Bible study that she and Kiser weren't having relations like the other ladies and their husbands. I just wonder if what Pastor Baker has isn't something nasty you pass around when you have relations, then it hides in your body and kills you slowly. I'm thinking that maybe those women got something from him, and then they may have passed it along to their husbands. If so, Kiser is one lucky man for not sleeping with his wife, but if he had something more than seventeen years ago, then I may be the unlucky one."

"Melvin, stop all of that nonsense and let's just forget about all of this. You are scaring me with your talk of leaving for a few days to think. Please put that bag up and go in there and kiss Peter good night. We love you so much, and we hate it when you leave us. You've never left the state without me."

"You know what Patricia, you are exactly right. God has truly blessed us. He brought us from a mighty long way. We have Peter, Mark and come next Sunday, we'll have our own church to lead. God is beyond awesome and I give him the praise and honor. Please forgive me for losing my temper. I will let this rest and leave it in God's hands. The saying remains true, what-so-ever goes on in the dark will come out in the light."

"Honey, you don't have to worry. I love my husband with all my heart. I know I have allowed Satan to temp me in the past, but not again. Since we got Peter, I've felt complete. We raised him as our own and I guess God saw fit to bless us with our own."

"Yes, I agree. I'm going to make sure that Peter is asleep and then I still must go. A few days away is exactly what I need to prepare my spirit for what's next to come."

"Sweetie, I'm just glad that you're not upset anymore. Peter, Mark and I will be fine right here until you get back. If you have time while you're out of town, pick me up a new dress and a big hat. I need to look extra special on Sunday as the new first lady of Deer Island Baptist."

As Melvin Riley finished packing his bag, he couldn't help but smile at how easy this situation had made it for him to slip away for a few days. In the past it was always a struggle trying to leave Deer Island without Patricia. She always felt as though she had to be glued to his hip.

Only Melvin knew that he wanted to get to Georgia ever since Paul left. Melvin has always questioned his sexuality since he was a young boy, but he didn't quite understand how he felt. He was always attracted to women but he had also noticed that certain men had given him a rise also. Melvin tried all he could to bury those feelings for good. He was successful until the night Paul came back for his mother's death. Paul had taken it so hard and it was Deacon Riley who consoled him. Somewhere in the crying and hugging things began to get out of control. It was when their face brushed against each other and the two men locked eyes that Deacon Riley knew he was in trouble. Paul initiated the kiss and Deacon Melvin Riley pushed him away. Paul then started apologizing and crying hysterically. Melvin embraced him again. This embrace was tighter than the first. Paul reached up and stroked Melvin's hair. Melvin didn't move so Paul gently planted small kisses on his lips before going in full force with his tongue forcefully.

Once the kissing got nice and sloppy, Paul made his move to take his action below Melvin's belt. At this point Melvin couldn't stop things if he tried. Both men's hearts were beating so hard it could be heard outside of their chests. Melvin had never imagined that being with another man could be more passionate than being with Patricia. Paul had indeed turned Deacon Melvin Riley out. If he could have seen himself, he would say that Paul had him climbing the walls. This was a feeling that he would chase over and over again. Paul had reassured him that their little secret was safe with him and if he could ever get away, the big city in Georgia was definitely the place to come.

Deacon Riley wanted to go and share his good news with Rev. Paul Kiser himself. He was sure that there was a celebration treat in store for him on the other side. Melvin couldn't believe his excitement over a man that he saw grow up from a baby. How did he let this happen to him? Especially after wondering how Pastor Baker could be such a slimy snake in the grass. Melvin wondered if his mix feelings for men and women were the reason why he forgave his wife and Pastor Baker for their betrayal so easily years ago.

Sylvia stood outside and listened to Mr. and Mrs. Riley's argument. She was boiling inside and couldn't understand why Mr. Riley backed down so easily, when he sounded so sure that he truly believed Mark wasn't his child. There were several times that Sylvia had to brace and contain herself from going in there and slapping Mrs. Riley across her face. She had never felt anything but goodness for this lady, but tonight the tides had turned for the worst. Sylvia knew that she was also feeling a lot of built up anger from past experiences that she had kept buried deep inside her. She hid behind the house as Mr. Riley got in his station wagon and pulled out his driveway. Sylvia figured that it was the God in him which allowed him to walk away from the situation so easily. For some reason it felt as though God had left Sylvia, because she felt like opening up a can of butt whipping on Patricia at the moment.

Sylvia's head was spinning and her eyes were red from the tears she had shed. She couldn't just go home, because she knew that there would be no rest for the weary. Sylvia started to think about Kiser, the hag, and Sarah. She had never fought a day of her life, but she figured that if she went into the Riley's house and Mark had John's face, she could put those three together and really mess things up pretty badly in there. Peter was down and Patricia was rocking Mark to sleep. Now was a better time than any other time to go in.

As soon as Patricia surfaced back to the front of the house alone, Sylvia barged in the front door which hadn't been locked since Mr. Riley left.

"I'm not here to play games Patricia. Let me see that baby. I have never disrespected you a day in my life. When Kiser gave y'all Peter, I never interfered. If I find out that you have disrespected me after all those talks that we had while John was gone about how much I loved him, it's going to be on. I want to see that baby right now!" yelled Sylvia.

"What's wrong Sylvia, why are you so upset? Mark is asleep." Patricia said.

"That's how I want to see him. I'm afraid to look the kid in the eye, afraid of what I might see."

"You can't just walk up in my house and demand to see my child!"

"Oh really, I'm going to see Mark alright." With this said Sylvia pulled Patricia aside and entered Mark's room. There was a lamp on near his crib. In the dim lighting, Sylvia saw what looked like Luke when he was about one month old. She blinked back the tears and when she turned around, she punched Patricia right in the nose. Then she straddled her and punched her some more. With each hit she yelled, "I hate you!"

Sylvia got home and felt like she had won this round. She looked at John and his two boys sleeping peacefully. Sylvia then looked around her house and compared it to the one that she had just left. She knew that most women in Deer Island would have traded places with her to be with Mr. John Jones. It wasn't John's fault that Patricia seduced him and jumped on him. He's a man. What man wouldn't taste the grace if you smothered him in it? Yet, it was hard for Sylvia to believe that this older lady had turned John on. John had to be drunk when he went over there to see about Peter, and didn't even know what he was doing. That's it, John was drunk. It was then that Sylvia knew she couldn't disturb her happy home. But for Patricia's betrayal, she was going to have to lose one son for another. Sylvia was taking Peter and she knew Patricia would do anything to protect her reputation, especially since she was about to become the new first lady. Too bad it would take more than makeup to cover her bruises. So it looked like Mrs. Riley would be missing next Sunday's church service after all. If not, she would have to explain to everybody how she got donkey kicked.

That night, pregnant and all, was the first time Sylvia had initiated sex with her husband. She felt like she owed it to him to learn how to please him. He was right when he said that she holds back from him. She had to find a way to let go of her past. John was not Kiser entering her. This is how she felt sometimes, especially when John would come to bed drunk. Tonight Sylvia planned to ride John like he was that old bull out in the green pasture. John was surprised himself when Sylvia stayed on for the full eight seconds, and she rode a little bit longer until her water broke.

Chapter 27

John was tired of looking out the window and seeing this big city. His body was tired and what he really needed was for Sylvia to come out of this coma and come back home. When Sylvia's water broke, she also had severe hemorrhaging. Neither John nor Sylvia knew what to do. Sylvia had a feeling that she had probably hurt her baby during her fight with Patricia. The pain grew intense and the blood continued to flow. John got Mr. Jones and his lady for the night to stay with the babies while he rushed Sylvia to the hospital. Once they got there, the doctors cut out her baby and Sylvia has been unconscious ever since.

Three weeks had gone by and Sylvia and baby David were still fighting for their lives. Baby David now weighed a little over a pound. He looked like a little alien as he held John's finger. No one was allowed to hold him because it was better for him to stay in his special enclosed case where he could keep warm and grow. David had entered this world almost four months before he was due. Sylvia had won the fight that night against Patricia, but because of it she was now losing her fight for life.

While David was getting stronger, Sylvia was getting weaker. Neither the doctor nor John could understand what went wrong with Sylvia and her pregnancy to cause this to happen to her. This

197

was her fourth baby and she had done well with all the others. For a matter of fact, this was the first baby to be born in a hospital. A midwife had delivered her other babies right there in Deer Island. Now Sylvia lied in a hospital bed with a huge cut below her belly button where they had pulled David out. John had seen many die during the war, but to watch Sylvia lying in a bed fighting for her life was way more than he could take. The doctors had informed them that her organs were now shutting down. They informed them that it was best to call other family members and let them know about Sylvia's situation just in case things turned out for the worst before morning.

Family members poured in to see Sylvia. The Joneses and Dunlaps came. John didn't realize how big Mary's family was until they all tried to squeeze into Sylvia's small room. Pastor Baker had come by in a hurry, stunned by the news. He had told Sylvia about him being her father the same night she fell ill, so he was blaming himself for her condition. He prayed for Sylvia and asked for her forgiveness. John then told him that it would be best if he left. John had no way of contacting Paul and knew that it would be devastating for him if Sylvia died without him being able to say goodbye to her. Mary's unexpected death was probably all that Paul could take for a decade. Mr. Tyson had tried the last number that Paul gave him, but those people didn't know of his whereabouts.

Before leaving Deer Island the day before, John had asked Joseph and his soon-to-be wife, which was also Joseph's step-sister, to stay at the house with his boys and Sarah. Mr. Jones and Mr. Tyson had helped out a lot with them and now they both needed to get other things done. John knew that he couldn't just let anybody stay with them because of Sarah. Sarah did not trust strangers and was very defensive toward them. She was also beginning to act rather strangely, especially when roaming around the house. John suspected she was trying to figure out where Sylvia was. Leaving Joseph with his boys was a very tough decision to make. John knew that if Sylvia knew that her boys were with Joseph, it would either kill her or wake her up from that coma. Sylvia had never shared with John what Joseph did while he was away, but after she had Luke and Matthew she had made it very clear to John that Joseph was to never be left alone with her children. John was confused because Joseph didn't act like a faggot and appeared to be very masculine. Paul on the other hand looked like he would bend over if a man tapped him on his shoulder. John didn't know what it was, but Sylvia had told him to never let her kids out of his eyesight when Joseph was around.

Sylvia also didn't know that Joseph was out of jail. Joseph had gone to jail just a couple of months ago for assaulting a man for whistling at his girlfriend. The poor guy that Joseph beat up knew that the lady was Joseph's step-sister but he had not heard about them being engaged to marry. Joseph busted the guy's head to the white meat. Joseph was only out of jail because Kiser's wife, Linda convinced Kiser to bail him out. Joseph had been locked up three times since John took Sylvia from their house. John knew that Sylvia didn't trust her brother, but John's hands were simply tied. Joseph was the only person that John could think of to leave in his house with Sarah. John made sure to explain to Joseph's girlfriend that she was to stay with the children at all times.

John could not understand why God was trying to do this to his family. He couldn't imagine his sons losing their mother at such an early age just as he had. He didn't want to be like his father and have to raise his offspring alone. Just when he thought he had it all, God was about to take his darling Sylvia from them. John had learned since being away in the military that it didn't matter how another lady looked or what she did to him, no other woman completed him like Sylvia. If Sylvia died right now, John knew that none of those ladies that had fulfilled his needs day after day in Deer Island when he left home to play could ever come close to completing him the way Sylvia does. Not even Patricia held a place in his heart. John just loved her for her goodies and conversation. He so hated it when Patricia had told him that she was pregnant. He felt like this was all Patricia wanted from the beginning, a baby, because soon as she told him that she was pregnant, she wanted nothing more to do with him. It was just too bad that Mark looked like him more than any of his other boys with Sylvia. John felt so stupid, because he had taken protective measures with all of the other women except Patricia to prevent this from happening. Patricia had convinced him that this was not necessary with her since she was unable to get pregnant. Hurting Sylvia was the very last thing that John wanted to do on this earth.

All of John's tears weren't helping Sylvia to wake up. John had cried and he had prayed, but Sylvia never responded. John kept asking the doctors and nurses if Sylvia could hear people when they spoke to her and they said that they didn't know for sure but it was best to keep talking just in case she could. They also warned him to be very careful what was said around her for the same reason.

John had promised Mr. Tyson that he would come back and pick him up later that evening. It was also best for him to go and check on everything at the house. John kissed Sylvia and sung

Sarah's favorite song to her before leaving hoping that she would think of her sister and realize her need to fight while he was away. John loved Sylvia and 'til death do us part would surely kill him.

When Sylvia was alone, was when Kiser snuck in to see her. At first Kiser just looked at her. Then he began to cry. He was so sorry for most everything he had done in his life. His acts toward Sylvia were one of the most that he was sorry for. It wasn't until he got help that he realized how screwed up he really was. His wife Linda had convinced him a year ago that the prison that he was in was far more worst than the jail Joseph had been locked up in. Linda had told Kiser that the hardest prison to escape was your own mind. Kiser was so thankful for having a wife like Linda. They could talk in a way that him and Mary never did. He felt like his beloved Sylvia had sent Linda to him to help ease his pain and to get him to go on with his life. He often wondered if Sylvia had found someone in heaven and was tired of him driving out there at night calling her name. So after his counselor advised him to stop driving out there at night to be alone, Kiser tried it.

Kiser had suffered from mental illnesses and would continue to have setbacks if he didn't take his medication. The doctor had told him that the abuse he suffered years ago along with witnessing Sylvia being raped and dying by the hands of her own father was enough to drive any man insane. Linda also talked Kiser into coming to church with her. She knew that Kiser would never sit in Deer Island Baptist unless it was another funeral he had to attend. So she took him to her church where she went before marrying Kiser. Linda was not from Deer Island but had come there one day to visit a friend. She had gotten lost and had stopped to ask Kiser for directions and this was when they met. She didn't know any of the stories that kept everyone else away from Kiser, which was Kiser's blessing from God. Linda had noticed Kiser's need for help quite early, but knew that she had to make him feel more comfortable with her first before talking about it.

Linda didn't pressure Kiser for sex. She stole Kiser's heart by being a mother figure to him and showed him love when he didn't want to be loved at all. She slowly began to see the changes in Kiser. When Kiser started to see the changes in himself and had repented for all of his sins, he just didn't know how to confront the people he had hurt. Then he heard about Sylvia being in the hospital with one foot already in her grave. He had to get here, but he had to be there alone with her. He looked around before speaking, not wanting to be heard like he was when he spoke to Doris at her grave.

Kiser grabbed Sylvia's hand and began to pray. "Dear Lord, I come to you again during my time of weakness. I am humble and depending on you Jesus. I ask you to end Sylvia's suffering and give her back to us while she still have breath in her body. Sylvia has always been a good child and she grew up to be a fine woman. I don't know her to have ever wronged nobody God. Jesus, I ask you to take me before you take Sylvia. I have no right to be here alive on this earth after all the wicked things that I have done. Please don't see fit for me to stay here and you take Sylvia. Her boys need her to be a mother. Lord, I know like nobody else how it affects you to lose a mother when you are just a kid. I don't want her boys to suffer the way that John and I suffered. I'm asking you to drive out all infirmity and sickness from her body. Please restore Sylvia to full health, dear Father. I have watched my Sylvia die before me.

Please don't allow my grandson to have to witness his Sylvia die also. I pray that you remove these curses from our lives that have been passed on from generation to generation. As you heal and renew Sylvia, Lord, may she bless and praise you. All of this I pray in the name of Jesus Christ. Amen."

Kiser continued to talk to Sylvia. "Sylvia, you've been through a lot. But you have to wake up from here and go home. Your children need you. Don't let them suffer without a mama to love them the way John and I did. At least John's father loved him. My father didn't know how to love me. I don't know what I did wrong. I tried to be tough like the Kiser men, but being tough was never enough for his love. One day he just told me that he was giving me my share of land and it was time for me to go. The day I left his property was the day that my family said goodbye to me. I've lived the rest of my life wondering where I messed up with my father. He didn't treat my brothers this cruel. So I assumed that it was what happened to me that day when I was raped by Sylvia's father that made him hate me. Sylvia, I'm sorry for what I did to you and our family. I just want you to know that I have gotten help. My wife Linda helped me to get through a lot of things, but I'm still a work in progress. The doctors told me that I have a mental illness that most likely stemmed from all the hateful things I endured in my past. It wasn't until I got help that I realized what I had done to you was immoral. I pray for Paul everyday that God would deliver him from his sissy ways and I've ask God to forgive me. If Paul ever comes back home, I will explain this to him. But you have to get up from here Sylvia. John needs you. Fight Sylvia, the Kiser curse must end." After saying all of this Kiser began to sob. He yelled out, "I wish that I never was a Kiser!"

"You are not a Kiser!" Mr. Tyson said as he and John walked in Sylvia's room.

"What?" John asked.

"Yes, y'all heard me right. We all have lived our lives with hidden secrets. George, you are a Tyson! I am your father." Mr. Tyson said.

"You are my father. How can you be my father? I am George Kiser, have always been George Kiser." Kiser said.

"Well, your mom and I had a little something going on a long time ago. You were the result of our love. You looked so much like her so we hoped that old man Kiser wouldn't suspect anything differently. He was beating her before she got pregnant with you and he continued to beat her. He was just a beater. I was a damn coward. I was such a coward that I was afraid until now to ever say anything. I knew that he would have killed me if he ever found out that I had stepped in on him. After your mother died, I knew that I was the only one that knew our secret, and I kept it to myself. There were times when I felt like he knew, especially when he gave you the land right across from my property. I saw how he treated you and he treated his other sons differently."

"So you mean to tell me that Kiser blood does not run through my veins? Do you know what this means and how my life could have been so different if I had known this years ago? I've always looked up to you as if you were my father Tyson. Why didn't you tell me after all these years? Even as a grown man it could have made life for everyone in my house so much better if you had just

204

said something. I did a lot of things the way I did it because I felt like a Kiser man had to do things a certain way. I hated being a Kiser for that same reason. I lived my life trying to please a father that couldn't be pleased by me. It took a lot of counseling for me to get to this point of understanding. I thank God for Linda coming into my life every day. She saved me from myself." Kiser said.

"I was a coward. I never married nor had another child because of how things went with you and your mother. I sat back over here and watched your place day and night. That's why I have always been around to help you in your times of need. I tried to be there for Sylvia too, because I felt sorry for her. I knew exactly when you lost your mind. Life messed you up. You never wondered why you and I could get along when no one else wanted to be around you. You didn't understand it, but I believe that you sensed that I was just as screwed up as you were. So son, it's not because you are a Kiser, it's because you really are a Tyson. Do know that we are who we are because of our bloodline, but there is more that goes in that than just who our mom, dad, and ancestors were. Our experiences with others and what we saw others doing also affects what we become. But we don't have to let any of that ruin us. We have choices and I'm glad to see that you, George have made a change. I love you my son and I love you too my great-grandson." Tyson said.

The three men stood hugging lightly shedding tears. When they looked up and turned around, Sylvia was looking at them with tears in her eyes. Sylvia spoke these words very weakly, "I've been washed by His blood and His blood has made me whole."

Chapter 28

Six Years Later
June 1985

It was hot and wet and I was ready to enter this cold bright world. I had swam around in the dark for too long, my days left inside here alive was numbered, if I didn't get out right now. I could hear the voices all around me and the tension was thick and gray. I could hear that familiar booming agitated voice that I had grown so familiar with. "You better hope that this one is a girl, cause I'm done! You've spat out four boys and I swear if this is another man-child, I'm pushing it right back up where it came from. I'm going to push it so far up your vagina; you are going to have a hysterectomy!"

My thought, "Here goes Mr. Fool again, didn't he know that I was special. I had heard this same talk month after month and knew that regardless of what I was at first, nothing was going to stop me from achieving my annual goal. Here I was healthy, vibrant, and most importantly female. I knew that the lady that would soon be known as my mother already had three grizzly sons and one runt of the litter. If she didn't have a girl this time, daddy was probably going to find someone who could. No one knew like I did, how much this man's life depended on having that one special daddy's little girl."

Sylvia was so happy to arrive at the hospital safely. John had driven like a fool for thirty-five miles to get them to the nearest facility. Sylvia was doing all she could to hold that baby in her. It felt like a foot was hanging through her lips but a quick wipe reassured her that it was just the mucous plug. "John, you really have to hurry or we are going to have a big clean up right here and it won't be on aisle nine, that's for sure."

"You better do all the praying that you can for the short while that you have left. You better be praying that she's all girl and beautiful at that. I'm getting sick and tired of feeding those lazy bastards that I already have at the house. Instead of a football team, I ended up with a five pound bag of couch potatoes. They won't do anything that you tell them to do until you call them and say 'Dinners ready.' I'm telling you Sylvia, that better be a girl in that there belly of yours or else."

"Or else what John? I've told you time and time again that they say you are the one responsible for determining the sex. Would you please stop hitting all those bumps, Jesus!"

"That's bull Sylvia! Have another boy and let's see who is responsible for determining the sex!"

"Thank God, we are here!" Someone grabbed Sylvia at the door, flung her in a chair and her feet left the floor. I knew that this was going to be the most special moment for her since the last decade. Sylvia and John's first son was born sixteen years ago when Sylvia was only twelve. They had been fooling around on the old man's plantation since Sylvia was nine years old and one day while lying on top of the pool table in the juke joint where Sylvia sold the man's moonshine, Pete was conceived. Pete was a big baby, nine pounds eleven ounces, her biggest baby yet. Pete was born at home, delivered by the community mid-wife. Yes, at twelve Sylvia pushed that baby out and to everyone's surprise; he was a hairy, hairy wooly thing.

I could hear someone yelling, "Push, push harder come on you could do it! You've done this four times already; let's go push that baby out of there! Keep pushing, keep pushing, it's coming!" After the yelling I could hear the moaning. Wow, I'm beginning to take a trip. Yep, I'm enjoying the ride; I'm getting out of here. Oops, what happened, I stopped, I'm not moving anymore. "Help, I can't breathe right here, somebody, anybody, do something!"

"I'm tired; I can't push, suppose it's not a girl. Then what will I do? I'm scared, Lord, help me, because I don't know what I'll do? Ouch!!!! It hurts so bad! Oh, Father Son and the Holy Ghost! Please forgive me for all the sins I've done!"

"Mrs. Jones, you have to push. You are putting your baby in great danger! Breathe! Breathe! Come on you can do it. I see the head! Push! Push! Push! There we go, there we go! Mrs. Jones, you have a GIRL!"

Crying, "A girl, I just had a girl! The Lord just blessed me, little old me with a girl! Thank you Jesus! Hey, somebody please go and tell John. This is the day that he's been waiting for, his girl, our girl, a beautiful, healthy girl."

Little that they knew, I was a special girl. One the world would never forget! Yes, created by God, birthed by man, living through a divine spirit.

John saw the man walking toward him. He didn't want to hear what the man had to say. He'd prepared himself already for the devastating news that he was about to hear. "Mr. Jones, you have a beautiful, healthy, girl!"

"What, did I just hear you correctly, I have a what?"

"You have a girl, yes, you and your wife finally have a beautiful girl."

John couldn't believe it after all these years, he was going to be able to take home one of life's most precious gift, 'Daddy's Little Girl.' She was all his and he would only give her the best of everything, starting today. So John left the hospital right away. "I sure can't take my baby home in that old Buick. New Cadillac here I come. You did it this time Sylvia!" John said.

Sylvia was a hot mess. She had definitely been on a roller coaster ride all day. One minute she was up and the next she was down, every now and again she felt like she was one inches from the ground. She would be right side up then upside down. "Where is John?" She had asked the nurse this fifty-eleven times that day. She couldn't believe it. Her baby girl had been born nine hours ago and neither one of them had seen John since she entered this world.

"Why did he do this to us?" Sylvia was crying her heart out. She loved this man, had known him all of her life as far as she could remember, but to this day, she didn't understand what made him tick. This was a man she gave her all too. She didn't have much, but she gave him her heart, trust, virginity, and she thought that she'd finally given him what he always expected from her, that precious, bright eyed special girl lying over there.

"Damn it John, you make me sick!" Sylvia lied there with her insides throbbing and sticky. She felt so dirty and couldn't wait to bathe. She still felt like she was bleeding a blood bath and if she kept feeling this way, she knew she would soon faint. Ten hours had past and still no John.

"Hey, baby. Where is she? Where is my baby girl?" Sylvia was awakened by John breathing down her neck. "I want to see her, let me see what I've created. I bet she is as precious as fine jewel, and as beautiful as the morning sunrise."

"Where have you been John? I can't believe you left us here! How could you leave here and not come see about your wife and kid? Are you really losing it? Sometimes when I think back of all of the off the wall things that you say and do, I truly believe that screws aren't as tight as they use to be. If your baby girl's life depended on you being here for us today, she would have been dead by now. So what if I told you that she didn't make it? Would you love me the same?"

"Sylvia, cut out the bull and tell me where my baby girl is! I don't have time for your drama. I've proven time and time again to you that I will always be here for you, so why doubt me now? I want only the best for my family, that's why I work so hard. I know that I've said a lot of stupid things lately, but it's just that since you told me you were pregnant again, and the doctor told you that you couldn't have any more kids, I totally lost it thinking about the possibility that this could be our 'God sent child.'"

"John, I know that you mean well. That's why I prayed without ceasing that God would bless us with a little girl for you to ruin, spoil, and love. I knew that your love for her would be unconditional and that she would be the glue that would hold our family together. Our precious angel is resting peacefully under the sound of our voices in the bassinet right over by the window."

"Oh, my God, she is beautiful. How did we create someone so special? I want to hold her, but I'm so afraid that I would want to just eat her up. These tears that I shed at this moment are tears of joy. Thank you Sylvia, you have given me everything that I've always wanted. I'm sorry that I upset you earlier. It's just that I want to make sure that my family is happy. On the way over here today, you kept fussing at me for hitting all of those bumps. I didn't want to tell you then because I didn't want to start an argument. I wasn't hitting any bumps, that was just how rough our car was riding. I thought about our ride over here and what I'd already put you and my little girl through and I said, 'It ain't nowhere in hell I'm putting my baby girl in that Buick for her first ride home to meet the boys! So, when I found out that it was a girl, I was so overjoyed that I ran out here to the nearest Cadillac dealership and bought my baby a brand new 1985 baby blue Cadillac. The teddy bear is for her too, but my love, she has to share that with all of you!"

"John, I'm so glad that you feel that way. There's something that I have to tell you, so listen. I know that in the Jones' family it has been custom for the fathers to name their babies. You've provided names for all of the boys and I see that all of their names came from the Bible. You even founded it necessary to name your son with Patricia, Mark. While you were gone I named our little girl and I hope that you will forgive me."

"You did what? You can't do that. I've already picked out the perfect name for her." John explained.

"John, I have named her Eve, because our little girl has already been cursed by our blood."

To Be Continued in the
sequel........

No Longer Broken

We are born into this world as free as we can be

We can't stand, walk, or talk

But our mothers' feel blessed that we can see

We look like slaves, heroes and some of us look like our ancestry

My oh my, what a shame when they say we must flee

I say, my ancestor was sold as a slave

It was his own tribe that tied him up and gave

To this day it's the white man we want to blame

He did nothing but sit back and got rich of our game

I am cursed, passed down by generations and it hurts

They say, do as I say, not as I do

If God chose you

Then he must have only chosen a selected few

You can preach, teach, and pray

And if we sit there you would do it all day

Come on Pastor who are you trying to fool

You know you are out there like a garden tool

I say, the word is there for us to read for ourselves

But we sit there with our Bibles on our dusty shelves

Yes, Pastor too is cursed

Most of what he says is rehearsed

It's because of past generations

And that can be researched

Can you really expect a man who was never loved to be able to love us

Especially when hate oozes out of him like a sore draining pus

He wants to have you as a good wife by his side

But everyone knows about the other women he goes in between
with the tide

Your son looks like him, her son looks like him

And you mean to tell me that no one has told them that they are
brothers

Could it be that he has brain-washed you, verbally abused you,

Got you to the point where you could care less about any of the
others

I say, a woman should concentrate more on making sure that the
boy

She gave birth to is love

Than trying to change that grown man she is sleeping with

And always praying for to our God above

Is it because of your mother, her mother,

And her mother's mother that we can't seem to get this right

Lord, if we don't break these cycles

We have already lost the fight

CURSED BY OUR BLOOD

Papa, Granny, Daddy, Mommy

Uncle, Auntie, even Barney

Have you touched us where you shouldn't

Then walked around pretending you didn't

I say, the torture was physically, emotionally, and mentally disturbing

You wonder why I sobbed

It was because I got robbed

I lost everything that I could have been

Now you have me living off of gin

And I wonder why I am cursed

Its because I blamed everyone except my next of kin

And to this day they don't realize that it was a sin

Cursed by past generations who did not repent is insane

Now we are praying and believing in God to break every chain

RUNWAY

I'm no longer cursed by our blood

Jesus rained on me and now I'm enjoying His flood

No longer cursed, No longer broken

Written By: Runway